Sunkissed

Also by Stephanie Ash

The First Kiss
One More Kiss

Sunkissed

Stephanie Ash

SPHERE

First published in Great Britain in 1998 by X Libris
Reprinted by X Libris 1999
This paperback edition published in 2012 by Sphere

A CIP catalogue record for this book
is available from the British Library.

ISBN 978-0-7515-5155-6

Typeset in Sabon by Hewer Text UK Ltd, Edinburgh
Printed and bound in Great Britain by Clays Ltd, St Ives plc

Papers used by Sphere are from well-managed forests
and other responsible sources.

MIX
Paper from
responsible sources
FSC
www.fsc.org   FSC® C104740

Sphere
An imprint of
Little, Brown Book Group
100 Victoria Embankment
London EC4Y 0DY

An Hachette UK Company
www.hachette.co.uk

www.littlebrown.co.uk

Sunkissed

Chapter One

Isn't it just sod's law, thought Anna.

Life with her long-term boyfriend Justin had been going about as smoothly as sandpaper for a couple of months; then, the night before she had to leave England to spend two months working on an archaeological dig in Crete, he seemed to have decided that he did love her after all and what's more, he wanted to prove it.

Anna couldn't help thinking about this latest disaster as she stirred two packets of sugar into the barely drinkable coffee she had just bought at the

Gatwick North terminal concession of some burger bar. The previous evening, Justin had finished work early, since it was to be their last night together for some time. He had made a special effort with the way he looked too, wearing Anna's favourite shirt, a soft green one he had had for years which brought out the colour in his gorgeous eyes, and, to go with the shirt, those great black jeans that made the most of his amazing bum.

Anna was more than a little embarrassed when she opened the door to Justin looking his best. All her decent clothes had already been packed away for the trip to Crete and she was wearing her oldest jeans and a T-shirt that had seen better days. Not that the stuff in her suitcase was so much better anyway. After all, there was little call for Armani in the life of someone who spent most of the year knee deep in mud or dust.

So Anna tried to make herself look presentable with a quick trip to the bathroom. She scraped her light brown hair back into a tidy high ponytail, framed her hazel eyes with mascara, and smeared on some deep plum-coloured lipstick while Justin waited in the hall. When she emerged, feeling just a little more butterfly than cocoon, Justin told her to let her hair loose again and take the war-paint off at once.

With Anna scrubbed clean once more, they walked to the restaurant hand in hand. They were only going to the pizza place on the corner of Anna's street – it did half-price offers on most nights – but it had been their special place at the beginning of their relationship when they were both still poor students. Now Justin was a rich City stockbroker whose biggest problem was in what colour he should order his new Porsche 911. Anna, however, was still quite broke, having decided to stick with archaeology rather than dump her vocation for a nine-to-five, overdraft-free existence in the 'real world', as Justin liked to term it.

As they walked to the restaurant, Anna noticed that they were talking carefully about Justin's day and not at all about hers. It was as though he still expected her to turn around and say that she had been joking, that she wasn't going away in the morning after all. Justin had tried to persuade her against spending the summer away from him but the Minoan history of Crete was a subject close to Anna's heart, and the opportunity to work on a major new Minoan site there was one that would become less and less frequent as ancient Greek theme parks with giant labyrinth-style waterslides and rollercoasters took priority over real history in the battle to attract tourism.

But Justin simply refused to understand. He said that Anna was going to Crete because she wanted to run away from him. Perhaps there was an element of truth in that, she thought as he said it for the fiftieth time. But not 'running away from', she decided; rather, he was pushing her away, for over the past few months Justin had become so wrapped up in the world of stocks and shares that little seemed to matter to him any more but the manufacture of money from money. Even when he wasn't at the office, it was still very much on his mind. Anna had noticed his attention drifting to his Blackberry when she talked to him about her work, where once he would have been rapt by her tales from the trenches. After all, archaeology had been his subject at university, too. He could talk for hours about Roman mosaics. But now it was as though he could no longer understand her having enthusiasm for anything that brought home less than fifty thousand pounds per annum, and sometimes Anna had to work hard to stop herself from being made to feel that perhaps what she was doing was slightly trivial compared to his work after all.

At the restaurant, they were shown to their usual table and they ordered their usual food. As Justin snapped the menu shut, Anna remembered how impressed she had been when they went to a Japanese restaurant shortly after Justin got his first real job after graduating. She had never eaten Japanese food before and so Justin had taken charge. He had ordered for her, telling her that he knew her well enough to know what she would like on that menu full of strange words that meant nothing to her. He had grown increasingly fond of being in charge after that. And not just in restaurants, but in bed, too. Moulding her body to his in a way that ensured not just his pleasure but her own.

At first she had enjoyed this change in him. Justin's high-flying City job had injected new confidence into all areas of his life. Anna remembered the thrill of being rushed upstairs from an important client's dinner party to be taken roughly from behind while hanging on to the edge of the hostess's chintzy dressing table. Justin's expression reflected in the mirror had been so determined, so confident, so powerful. The Justin she had met at college would have been far too worried about causing offence to take the risk of being caught *in flagrante*. Justin the City boy just didn't care.

But now things were different again. Anna too had changed, and she was no longer the meek creature who had been grateful for Justin's continued attention in the face of all those City temptations. Deciding to take the job in Crete had been a turning point for her. It was a sign to herself that she was going to start taking her career every bit as seriously as Justin took his. The confidence her new employers had shown in taking her on had started to rub off on her attitude.

To be honest, the thought of getting on a plane and flying out to meet a couple of complete strangers for a month on an island where her knowledge of the local language was limited to 'please' and 'thank you' filled her with something approaching terror, but Anna hoped that she would survive the experience and come out stronger than before. She prayed that the same could be said for her relationship with Justin.

Meanwhile at the restaurant, the food had finally arrived. They bolted it down and soon it seemed that Justin was calling for the bill before Anna had decided that she didn't really want coffee. His hand was already on her knee beneath the table and even under the shadow of her imminent departure, the passion between them was breaking through the strain.

'Let's go straight to bed, eh?' Justin had said as, a very hurried walk home later, Anna pushed open the door to her flat. She didn't argue, but let him back her into the bedroom, stripping off their clothes as they went, leaving a trail of his and her garments behind them like scattered petals. Once in the room, Justin placed his hands on her shoulders and gently pushed her down on to the unmade bed. Level with his waist, Anna wrapped her arms around him and covered his taut, toned belly with gentle kisses before moving slowly down his body to where his hard-on already bobbed to attract her attention.

'I don't want you to go,' he murmured hotly into her long silky hair.

'I know,' she said. 'But don't let's think about it now. We've got ages until morning.'

She reached up to pull him down on top of her. Justin nuzzled his mouth against the side of her satin-soft neck, savouring the smell of her delicious perfume as though this might be his last ever chance to smell it. Anna twisted her fingers in his thick blond hair and sighed as he moved his attention further down her body, kissing a trail from her porcelain neck down to her beautiful breasts, greeting each of the perfect hemispheres with a kiss as though they were old friends.

Sighing, Justin cupped a delicate pink breast in each hand and brought them together, burying his face in the deep cleavage he made between them. Now Anna sighed too, as Justin moved to tongue her waiting nipples into hard pink peaks. Then he nipped at them, carefully, until she thought she might squeal with excitement. Justin could always press the right buttons in the bedroom. He knew Anna's body almost as well as she knew it herself.

'I love it when you do that,' she told him as he suckled at her breast. He obliged by doing it slightly harder. Anna drew in breath sharply and ran her hands up Justin's back, scratching urgent pink pathways on his smooth brown skin with her long fingernails. Justin arched his back in response. His eyes were closed and his mouth already stretched wide into an ecstatic smile.

Then Justin moved down her body again. This time, he hesitated around her waist, first gently tracing the outline of her navel with his tongue, then probing at it, penetrating it, until she began to squirm. Down below his kisses, Anna could already feel herself becoming aroused, her vagina getting wetter and warmer in response as Justin circled her belly button. After a while, she had to push him away again, giggling as she did it, to get him to concentrate on the areas that really mattered.

Justin slipped down from the bed and knelt before her on the floor. Putting a hand on each of Anna's knees he parted her legs so that she lay fully exposed to him. Teasingly, he began to lick at the bottoms of her tiny narrow feet. As he tickled, Anna curled in her toes and squirmed in a vain attempt to avoid his tongue, but he had a hand on each of her ankles now and she knew that he wouldn't let her go until he wanted to.

'Don't tickle me,' she begged him. 'Do something more exciting.'

Rising to the challenge, Justin slid his hands up her calves, following close behind them with his mouth, kissing a damp path along the inside of her legs until his hot lips reached the tops of her thighs. Anna's hands rested delicately on her pubic bone. Justin moved them away with his chin and nuzzled his face in her glossy pubic hair.

'Oh, yes,' Anna sighed. 'Yes. Do that. That's good.'

His darting tongue had found her clitoris, already swollen and quietly aching for his attention. He flicked the little nub from side to side with his strong pink tongue, then sucked it between his lips as though it were a miniature penis. Nipping gently at the tiny nub with his perfect teeth, he drew a sharp breath from Anna above.

He slipped his hands between her thighs again, this time finding her labia and parting them carefully like a fisherman expecting to find a pearl. On the bed, Anna twisted luxuriously in anticipation of the feeling of his tongue on those other lips. Her vulva already glistened with the juice of her desire for him, ready to mingle with his saliva and make her wet enough to take him in easily in one ecstatically welcome stroke.

Justin delicately caressed the shining pink lips of her vulva with his mouth. The warm musky scent of her body filled his lungs, mixed tantalisingly with the heady tropical flower perfume of the body lotion she had smoothed on to her thighs in preparation for this last precious evening together. Justin stretched out his tongue and probed deep inside her, holding her thighs steady so that she couldn't roll away and escape.

'Take me now,' she begged him when she thought that she might break down and come before he even got anywhere near her.

But she needn't have worried, because Justin was more than ready. He moved up the bed until he was lying directly on top of her, then slid his hand down between their hot bodies and guided his stone-hard penis between her legs and her slippery labia. Anna drew breath sharply at the first thrust, quickly relaxing again when she felt his pelvis touch hers. Then, sighing deeply, she thrilled to the singular joy of being filled so completely and expertly by his shaft.

Justin gazed at her face steadily as he began to move, holding himself high above her body with his strong arms. Anna's own gaze wandered over the taut muscles of his arms and his chest. It was as though she were trying to take in a picture of him that would keep her feeling close to him all the time she was away. A picture of the way that his pumping veins bound his hard muscles like tightly wrapped cord. A picture of the powerful flex of his pectoral muscles as he moved forward above her and took all his weight on his beautiful arms.

Next she switched her attention to his pelvis, to the way he was thrusting slowly in and out of her, so that their bodies appeared like two parts of a fantastically well-oiled machine. To Anna the sight of Justin's dick plunging into her was almost as good as the feeling it gave her deep inside. She felt her vagina begin to pulse in appreciation of him with the first stroke. It was a steady, rhythmic pulse that began to spread slowly throughout her limbs like the spring sun melting ice.

Justin knew exactly what she wanted. He always had done. When he was sure that she was almost unbearably aroused, he began to change the direction and depth of his thrusts. Whether he was aiming straight for her G-spot or just tickling at the edges of her labia with the very tip of his shaft, each and every stroke was carefully calculated to drive her completely wild.

Anna lifted her legs from the bed and wound them tightly around Justin's body, at the same time grasping his buttocks with her hands and using them to bring him further inside her still. Her fingers dug hard into his soft warm flesh as she grew more and more excited, forcing him to increase the pace of his movement to keep time with her racing breath.

'Do it harder,' she told him huskily. And he responded instantly. His teeth were gritted together in ecstatic determination as he thrust into her powerfully with strokes that hammered against her swollen clitoris and drove her to the edge. Deep down inside, she had the sensation of reaching the very top of a rollercoaster. Her stomach suddenly seemed to flip over inside her and for a moment she felt quite weightless as her orgasm set in and quickly took hold of every nerve in her shaking body.

She was coming long before him. Her vagina contracted and throbbed around his penis as though she were trying to pull him inside her for always. Justin continued to thrust, his face smiling down on her face. Anna's eyebrows were tipped together in concentration but her mouth was spread in a wide, wide grin.

'Come, you bastard,' she shouted as joy racked her body and set her all a-shiver. 'Come with me now.'

Justin pushed against her once more and this time he stayed there, held tight against her body as his orgasm took off too. Anna opened her eyes just in time to see him coming. Just in time to see his composure disappear completely as his thrusts became uncontrolled and a groan he could no longer hold inside exploded from his mouth.

'I'm coming!' he yelled.

She already knew. She could feel it. She could feel the powerful spasm of his penis as it shot his sperm deep inside her again and again and again. Riding his climax, Anna clung to Justin's body as though if she let him go he might float off into space and be lost to her for ever. Her vagina pulsed in time with his spasms. She wanted the orgasm to go on and on and on.

When Justin had finished, he collapsed on top of her, panting for air. Anna wrapped her arms around his back and held him close, keeping him inside her while they tried to catch their breath. She closed her eyes and savoured the sensation of his penis still hard between her legs, until it began to go soft again and slipped slowly from her vagina, leaving a trail of warm, wet, sticky semen on the inside of her shaking thigh.

She sighed when Justin finally rolled away from her. They hadn't made love so passionately in ages, and though she knew that the passion had been more than slightly fuelled by anger and frustration on Justin's part, Anna felt happier than she had done in a long while.

'You don't have to go.' Justin traced a line up the inside of Anna's arm as they lay side by side in her bed later that night. She didn't know whether it was an observation or an order.

'I *do* have to go. It's an important job,' she said for the thousandth time since she had first got the email confirming her success. 'The position is a recognition of all the hard work I put into my doctorate. And I need the money.'

'Well, for heaven's sake, Anna,' Justin replied quickly, seeing his moment and doing his best to seize it. 'Why didn't you tell me that before? Money doesn't have to be a problem, you know. I could pay you to stay here. How about that?' He grinned widely. As far as he was concerned, he had just found the answer to all their problems.

'You could pay me to stay here?

'Well, I could loan you some money until you find something nearer.'

'Justin, I think you're missing the point,' Anna told him patiently. 'Why don't you pay yourself to fly out to Crete to see me instead?' She smiled. 'It'd be a nice break for you. You need a holiday. A couple of days in the sunshine. Sea, sand. Lots of cocktails. What do you think? I could get some time off from the dig too . . . We could hire a car or something. Explore the island. It'd be fun.'

'You know I'll be way too busy for that,' Justin said flatly.

Of course he would. Anna turned her face away from him. There was no way that anything so trivial as visiting his absent girlfriend could warrant Justin having a long weekend or taking even one day off from his precious job. After all, the money markets of the world would surely collapse without him. Anna had to bite her lip to stop an outburst of sarcasm on that particular point.

Justin leaned up on his elbow and stared down into Anna's shadowed face. 'Are you trying to prove something to me by doing this Crete thing?' he asked. 'Is that it? Do you think I can't manage without you?

Because I can, you know. I can manage very well on my own. It's just that I don't want to have to.'

'It's not that,' Anna began cautiously.

'Do you want more commitment? Is that it?' Justin interrupted.

'I—'

'Is that what it would take to stop you going away . . .'

Anna snorted. 'Did you just ask me to marry you, Justin?' she joked.

'No,' he said. 'But if you decide to stay here instead of going off on some stupid boring dig, then we could talk about moving in together, I suppose. What do you say?'

Justin was already downgrading his proposal. 'I'm not even going to bother answering that question. You don't mean it, Justin. They're the words of a desperate man. I am going to Crete. And you're not going to persuade me otherwise by pretending that you want anything more than we already have. I'll only be gone for two months, for heaven's sake. It's not as if I'm leaving for ever.'

'A lot can happen in two months,' Justin said threateningly.

'I assure you that nothing will.'

'Call me when you know the right answer to my question, Anna,' he persisted. 'But don't wait too long or the offer may be retracted.'

'Then it could hardly have been an offer made in love, could it?' Anna retorted angrily. 'Besides, I'm still not sure what you were actually offering. Look, if you really want me to be with you for the rest of your life, surely you can spare me for just two short months.'

Suddenly Justin got up and began to search the floor around the bed for his pants, leaving Anna shivering on the mattress where he had whipped the duvet away in his hurry.

'What are you doing now?' she asked him in exasperation as she clawed back the covers.

'I'm going home, that's what I'm doing. You've made it quite clear that you don't care whether I'm here with you or not, Anna, so I'm not going to waste any more of your precious time. Or mine.'

'What do you mean? I didn't say that. Get back into bed, Justin. Please. It's our last night together . . .'

'Exactly. Our last night,' he spat. Justin found his pants and started to pull them on, but he was so wired up that he didn't notice that he was putting a leg through the waistband. Anna couldn't help laughing as he started to hop about like a cartoon cowboy with his chaps in a twist.

'I think you might want the leg-holes,' she told him calmly.

But Justin couldn't see the funny side. Correcting his mistake, he pulled up his pants so quickly that he might have snapped his dick off had it been in the way. Within seconds he was fully dressed, lacing up his shoes and giving Anna one last chance to 'come to her senses' before he left for good.

'Why don't you drive me to the airport tomorrow morning?' she asked him patiently, in an attempt to find another way to say that she was going and that was that. 'We can talk about all this on the way.'

'Why don't you call yourself a taxi?' he replied.

Then, without kissing her goodbye, Justin left the flat like an angry tornado. But it was a while before Anna heard him start his car. Perhaps he had been giving her the chance to run outside and stop him leaving. Anna sat up in bed and looked thoughtfully at her mobile on the little table beside her. She could easily call him. Tell him to stop being so silly and come back upstairs so that they could kiss and make up.

Anna picked up the phone, but before she had dialled the last digit of Justin's number she changed her mind. To call him now would be to admit that she was in the wrong – and perhaps it was time he realised that there were things in her life that were almost as important to her as the stock market so obviously was to him. So, instead of calling him, Anna rolled over on to her side with a sigh, and tried in vain to get some sleep. He would be bound to call in the morning anyway. He would want to say goodbye to her properly. Wouldn't he?

Chapter Two

'Wake up. Wake up!' Someone was shaking Anna by the shoulder. 'You haven't got time for a nap now, Sleeping Beauty. They're boarding our flight at Gate 12.'

At the sound of the unfamiliar voice Anna opened her eyes to see the pretty, round face of Miranda Sharpe, her new colleague. They had met briefly while checking in, but then Miranda had raced off to make a few last-minute calls to her university department colleagues to ensure that some important tasks would be done while she was away, leaving Anna to succumb to the sleep she had missed while worrying all night about that argument with Justin. He still hadn't texted or called, despite the fact that she had caved in and texted him three times.

But as Miranda had said, the airline was indeed starting boarding procedures for flight number CK954, and by the time the two of them reached the departure lounge, a queue snaked all the way back from the passport control desks to the door.

'No expense spared, eh?' sniffed Miranda, referring to the fact that they were flying out to their new job cattle class with dozens of tattooed tourists, off to find the best egg and chips in the sun. 'Bet old Sillery didn't have to fly out to Crete like this,' Miranda continued. 'Bet they hired a bloody Learjet for him.'

'I heard he has his own,' Anna replied.

Doctor William Sillery was to be their new boss. He was head of the archaeology department at a prestigious red-brick university and Britain's number one expert on Ancient Minoan civilisation. Academically, he was brilliant as a diamond, but his books on the subject were as dry as day-old toast. Anna remembered with a shudder wading through Dr Sillery's *Secrets of Ancient Greece* fuelled by gallons of coffee, and quoting him wholesale in her final undergraduate exams. She hoped that working with him would prove to be a little more fun than that particular period of her life had been.

'Have you ever worked with Dr Sillery before?' Anna asked Miranda.

'What? Oh, yes,' Miranda said with a strangely ominous tone. 'Doctor Sillery and I were together in Cyprus last year. What a scream that was, I can tell you.'

'Is he a slave-driver?'

'Makes Stalin look like a real pussy cat. It was the dig from hell.'

'So why are you putting yourself through it again? Sucker for punishment?'

'Something like that. Though I don't think it's me who'll be punished this time,' she added mysteriously. 'Anyway apart from Sillery, last year I was lumbered with Giles Dawkins. Have you met him?

He's an Oxford university man. Anglo-Saxon specialist actually, so I'm not quite sure what he was doing with us. He had this huge beard that always had bits of food stuck in it. Toast crumbs here. Fish-tail there. Really gross. And, I swear, open-toed sandals were invented especially for him. You have never seen such disgraceful toenails. You look like you'll be more fun, though.' Miranda cast an unashamed eye over Anna's thigh-hugging jeans and close-fitting T-shirt.

'Well,' said Anna shyly, self-consciously crossing her arms across her chest and scrunching up her pink painted toes in her Birkenstocks. 'I hope I won't disappoint you. I don't feel all that much like having fun at the moment.'

'Let me guess,' Miranda sighed dramatically. 'You're leaving some special someone behind?'

'Is it that obvious? How did you know?'

'Because that's always the problem with the girls who come on these trips. They're always mooning about the wonderful boyfriend they had to leave back home. No doubt you've got his picture set as the wallpaper on your phone and you'll be getting it out to kiss it every time my back is turned. I mean, I'm always leaving someone behind too, but since I never intend to go back to them it doesn't really matter to me.'

'Really? Who are you deserting this time?' Anna couldn't resist asking.

'The son of a bitch who got me this job, as a matter of fact,' Miranda replied dryly. 'He's off to Cornwall this summer with his wife and 2.5 children, and he wanted to be sure that I would be safely out of the way. Unfortunately, Crete was about as far out of the way as he could manage.'

'Oh. That's rough,' said Anna, sensing a hint of disappointment in the other girl's revelation.

'Yeah, well. You don't take a book out of the library if you don't think you'll be able to give it back, do you?'

The queue shuffled forward half an inch.

'Let's hope I meet something that'll take my mind off him in sunny Crete, eh?' Miranda continued.

'Something?' Anna repeated with amusement.

'Well, it probably won't be William Sillery from what I've heard of him. Are we the only other people going on this dig?'

'I don't know,' said Miranda. 'I mean, I think we are,' she added distantly.

Anna began to ask her new friend what Dr Sillery had found at the site so far, but Miranda's attention had already been diverted and she was swapping coy glances with a young guy wearing a Manchester United T-shirt, who was carrying a fully inflated crocodile-shaped lilo beneath a tattooed arm. When he got to passport control, he was told that he would have to let the lilo down before he took it on to the plane. Miranda giggled as he turned and appealed to her for sympathy like an unhappy clown.

'Hope we get to sit next to him,' said Miranda.

Anna thought out loud, 'I hope we don't.'

Fortunately it was Anna's wish that was granted. Miranda's fancy piece was seated towards the back of the plane, while the girls were seated together over the wing. For fifteen joyous minutes, as the plane gained its cruising height, Miranda and Anna talked seriously about the dig and its potential. Anna knew that beneath her fluffy exterior, Miranda had a brain like a brand new razor and they were supposed to be forming an academic crack team for this important job. But then the seatbelt sign went off and dinner was served. The unnaturally handsome steward attending to the girls was obviously gay, but that didn't stop Miranda from batting her eyelids when he poured the tea and squeezing past him quite deliberately on an unnecessary trip to the loo.

'Good for practising your oral skills on,' she explained when Anna suggested that she might be wasting her time. 'Just talking, I mean. Though everything I know about blowjobs I learned from a gay guy, too. Straight men are too shy to tell you what they really want in bed but when you talk to a gay guy, it's just like talking to another girl. It was very enlightening. Can you believe that up until I was eighteen, I actually thought that you literally had to blow? I went puffing up and down my boyfriend's dick like it was a hot sausage.' She demonstrated on a stuffed finger roll from the in-flight meal. 'It never occurred to me to put the thing right in my mouth and suck it.'

'Really.' Already Anna thought that coming from Miranda that statement seemed startlingly naive.

'No,' Miranda guffawed as she popped an after-dinner mint into her mouth in one bite. 'But Lawrence – that's my gay best friend – did tell me this great tip about flicking the raphe. That's the little bit of skin that joins the foreskin to the shaft. You know where I mean? Anyway, you just flick that back and forth with your tongue. Guaranteed to drive all men absolutely insane. Never fails.'

'I must remember that.' Anna tried to concen-trate on the papers that Dr Sillery had sent them as preparation, but Miranda hadn't finished.

'And loads of ball-fondling simultaneously. They come in seconds if you do that too. Very valuable tips indeed. You need never have lockjaw again.'

Anna smiled tightly. She had caught the middle-aged man in the seat in front craning to hear more, obviously wondering if he had a raphe himself. Now his wife was giving him a slap on the arm to draw his attention back to the official in-flight entertainment – some ancient chick-flick. No wonder he found the girls' conversation more interesting.

'I think I might try to get some sleep,' said Anna tactfully, before Miranda had a chance to turn the recycled air in the plane completely blue.

'Oh, OK.' Miranda looked pretty disappointed to have lost her audience so soon in the flight, but Anna closed her eyes regardless. Though now she couldn't actually sleep because her mind was domi-nated by the faintly disturbing image of a great bobbing shaft, candy pink and glistening with semen, that just begged to be sucked. Anna smiled at the thought. It might beat counting sheep . . .

In her mind's eye, Anna could see her own hand as she wrapped her slim fingers around this proud imaginary member, which was attached to heaven only knows who. Slowly, Anna moved her closed fist up towards the penis head. Then down again, towards the balls. Faster and faster she worked, increasing the pressure little by little each time she moved her hand. As she imagined this exercise, the rest of the body of her mystery lover began to become more clear. Now she could see the tightly curled blond pubic hair winding up across his abdomen on to a rock-hard, well-tanned belly. She traced the line of hair up to a perfect belly button, which was resting in the centre of a set of stomach muscles that could have stopped a bouncing bomb.

Anna took her hands from the penis and began to run them slowly up this fast-forming body. She leaned forward and kissed the tanned tight, hard pectoral muscles which were covered by just a smattering of soft yellow hair. She breathed in and could smell the musky, manly scent of his sweat. She flicked out her tongue and could taste him. His skin was salty and yet strangely sweet. High above her head in her daydream, Anna could hear the soft sound of his breathing. He was moaning just a little as she took one of his tiny nipples between her sharp teeth and pulled.

The vision now had arms of his own, and hands that came down on her shoulders and pulled her back from his chest and towards the bobbing shaft. Anna complied willingly, taking the shaft in her hand again and then dipping her head towards it. She pulled back the silky foreskin so that the throbbing pink helmet was now completely exposed. She could see the raphe that Miranda had described, delicately connecting the soft foreskin to the shaft. Anna stretched out her tongue languorously so that her lover knew exactly what she intended to do before she even began. Above her, a breath was sharply drawn. She leaned forward and touched the shiny pink dome with the tip of her tongue, flicking away the glistening drop of semen that had gathered there as she hesitated.

The hands on her shoulders gripped tightly as she began to work on her dream lover in earnest, flicking her tongue from side to side and gently taking the raphe with it each time. She kept the foreskin held tightly back so that the most sensitive part of the penis was always exposed. Her dream lover groaned as she drew her hot pink tongue across the shining eye of his shaft. Then she moved one hand down to his balls and cupped them gently, drawing her fingers together beneath them as though she were stroking the chin of a cat.

Her lover's fingers twisted agitatedly in her hair; then suddenly he was holding the back of her head, forcing her further towards him still. But Anna wasn't going to take him right into her mouth yet. She wanted to tease him just a little more. She wanted to drag him right to the edge of desire and leave him dangling there for as long as he could hang on with her.

'Anna,' he whispered. 'Anna, you're driving me crazy. Anna, don't do this to me!'

She didn't recognise the voice. But then what could be more exciting than possessing the body of a tall handsome stranger?

'Anna, could you hold this for me?'

The grip of his hand on her forearm was so real-istic. It was almost as if he were there with her on the plane.

'Anna! Wakey-wakey, dream girl. Will you hold

this for me while I pop to the ladies' again? Must have had too much coffee.'

Pop went the dream bubble. It was Miranda. She needed to squeeze past into the aisle of the plane and wanted Anna to hold on to her cup.

'What?' Anna sprang upright in surprise and for a moment didn't even know where she was. She just about managed to take the proffered coffee cup without spilling the lot while Miranda escaped into the aisle. When Miranda came back again, she was smiling like the Cheshire cat.

'You were talking in your sleep, you know. Or rather moaning,' she added. 'I do hope we're not going to have to share a room.'

Chapter Three

Dr Sillery didn't meet the girls at Crete's Heraklion airport as he had promised. Their flight had been delayed and he had sent a driver and his apologies so that he could get on with the important business of his beauty sleep while Anna and Miranda struggled unaided through the undermanned passport control. They might have stayed at the airport all night had Miranda not noticed a surly-looking driver with a cardboard placard bearing the legend 'Ann and Manda' in a spidery scrawl. When almost everyone else from their flight had been packed on to various tour operators' courtesy buses, the girls finally realised who 'Ann and Manda' must be, and reluctantly followed the driver to his battered old car.

After a journey that took them far too close to the edge of several mountain roads, the girls were spectacularly relieved to reach their destination and only a little disappointed to find that no one was waiting up to meet and greet them. Fortunately, they didn't have to share rooms. There were two to choose from. Anna found herself taking the one on the ground floor, since Miranda claimed to be afraid of people climbing in through her window to molest her during the night – despite the fact that she had spent most of the taxi journey there saying how much she was looking forward to getting some action with a tall dark stranger if there were any tall dark strangers to be had.

Alone at last, Anna sat down on the bed and checked her phone again. Of course, she had switched it back on the second the plane touched the tarmac but only to be disappointed to see that

Justin still hadn't been in touch. Now, to her horror, Anna discovered that there was no signal in her new mountainside abode. She tried switching her phone on and off again, to see if that made any difference. It didn't. She tried leaning out of the window. She tried standing on the bed, holding the phone as near to the ceiling as possible. No joy. If Justin had relented, she wasn't going to know about it that night. That wasn't going to stop her thinking and worrying about him, however.

Anna had expected to lay awake half the night, but in the end she fell asleep the moment her head hit the pillow. The combination of that last sleepless night in London without Justin and the uncomfortable flight to the island had worked its magic on her better than any sleeping tablet. But the sleep wasn't quite as long as she might have hoped for. At dawn, a feisty cockerel in the yard outside her window began its rude wake-up call. Anna jerked upright in her bed and for several moments did not have a clue where she was or what she was doing there. Then she saw her suitcase standing like a sentinel by the door and remembered. She was in Crete. She was a pretty long way away from home. And from Justin.

She padded to the square window of her room and drew back the thin white curtains, which were much less effective at keeping out sunlight than mosquitoes. At first, she could see hardly anything because of the bright sun outside, which seemed to be shining directly in her eyes, but gradually the view became clear. And what a view it was. During the pitch-dark ride up to the villa, Anna had lost all sense of direction. But now she could see that they had travelled due east along the main highway that hugs the coastline of Crete towards the pretty little fishing village of Agios Nikolaos. The clear blue sea glittered on the horizon, dotted with tiny fishing boats like jewels. To her left and to the right of her rose barren-looking mountains that tumbled and crumbled their way down to the beach. Breathing in deeply, Anna could almost smell the salt on the rippling waves.

It certainly beat looking out through the window

of her Camden flat on to the dustbins of the flat below, she thought.

Anna wondered if anyone else was awake. She could hear no recognisable sounds but the insistent crowing of the irritating cockerel and the distant stirring of the sea. Slipping on her newly bought sandals, Anna crept out of her room and tried to find a door that would lead her outside into the garden. Once there, she sat down on the shining front step of the villa, taking in a wider view and marvelling at the incredible heat of the sun, which had already made the stones beneath her bare feet warm to touch.

'Beautiful,' she murmured. Fragrant pink flowers tumbled like a waterfall from a cluster of terracotta pots beside the house. As her eyes became accustomed to the light, she could make out a tiny, white painted church with a blue roof sitting high on a hill to the west. The Cretans always built their churches on hills in the theory that the high ground was nearer to God. The gentlest of breezes lifted her fringe from her face like a lover's cooling kiss. And Anna was in love with the place already.

Pretty soon though, the cockerel must have got to everyone. Anna heard the sound of a window being opened above her, then footsteps pattering across the marble floor of the hallway behind her. She turned to find out who was creeping up on her, unable to see too much in the shadows because of the bright sun that had been burning into her eyes.

Gradually, two sandalled feet came into view. Anna followed the legs up to the knees. Very hairy, and obviously male. Then she shaded her eyes and looked up at the stranger's face with an especially welcoming smile. Better look friendly, she thought. It might be Doctor William Sillery, the irascible don.

'You are up very early,' the stranger said. No hint of irascibility in that voice. 'You should ignore Georgios for as long as you want to. It is Sunday, after all.'

'Georgios?'

'Yes. The bird,' said the stranger. 'The man chicken.'

'The man chicken?' Anna smiled. 'You mean the cock, I think. And you are?'

'Vangelis,' said the stranger. 'My name is Vangelis Georgiadis and I am your host at this villa.'

Anna struggled to her feet and dusted herself off. 'I'm Anna,' she said, thrusting out her hand in greeting. 'Anna Hazel. I'm with the dig.'

'Anna,' Vangelis repeated carefully, shaking her hand hard. 'I've heard a lot about you. And read some of your work, of course.'

Anna couldn't help blushing at the thought. 'I hope it didn't send you to sleep.'

'Oh, no. I was very interested. You have some fascinating theories on the Minoan age. I am very sorry we couldn't wait for you at the airport last night. But your plane was so late and Dr Sillery was very tired after his first day at the site.'

'That's OK. I understand. Did he find anything exciting yesterday?'

'Not yet,' said Vangelis. 'But Dr Sillery will tell you more about that when you see him. Come and join me for breakfast first. If you are hungry . . .'

'Hungry? I'm ravenous!'

Anna eagerly followed Vangelis through the house

to the back yard where the sun was still bright but not right in her eyes. As they walked, he explained the house rules to her in impeccable English. No toilet paper down the loos of course, or she would block up the whole of the dilapidated Cretan sewage system. And the water in the bathroom was solar heated. So she must never expect it to be really hot.

On the table in the back yard, Vangelis had already laid out breakfast. There was orange juice, toast, thick creamy Greek yoghurt with golden swirls of honey. Anna was starving. The Cretan plumbing may have left a lot to be desired, but at least they could do good food.

Vangelis pulled out a seat for her, then took his place opposite. Now that her eyes had recovered from the glare and she could see properly again, Anna was surprised to discover that her host looked much younger than his voice had sounded. He was in his late twenties, perhaps. Early thirties at the very most. He had thick dark hair that hung in shaggy corkscrew curls to his shoulders. And what shoulders they were, hewn straight from polished marble and shown off to perfection by his faded blue vest. Anna surreptitiously clocked her host's dreamy brown eyes as he concentrated on pouring out coffee, and wondered how long she had to get to know him before Miranda turned up and decided that this one was hers.

'I am very happy to have you all staying here at my house,' Vangelis was saying. 'I am very interested in Dr Sillery's work here. It is important that we save as much of Crete's past as we can before they start to build the hotel.'

'Of course, the hotel.' Anna remembered hearing that they had just two months to work on the site before the owners of the land started to construct a new three-hundred-room hotel, with two vast heated outdoor swimming pools.

'Are you helping at the dig?' she asked.

'Of course I am,' Vangelis said through a mouth full of toast. Anna smiled. His presence would undoubtedly render Miranda pretty much useless. 'I studied archaeology in Athens. I specialised in what we are hoping to find here in Crete . . .'

At that moment, Miranda appeared. Unlike Anna, she had taken care to make sure she looked her best before she came down for breakfast. She was dressed in a loose-fitting white dress that seemed to have no structure to it at all, and yet somehow managed to show off every curve of her gracefully generous body to the best possible effect. She had piled her blonde hair up in a loose chignon that emphasised the downy length of her delicate neck, and coloured in her rosebud lips with just a little smudge of pinky-red lipstick.

'My goodness, isn't it hot out here?' she sighed to no one in particular, flapping the neckline of her dress dramatically so that Vangelis had the full benefit of her cleavage. 'You must be Vangelis,' she said, squeezing herself on to the bench beside him. 'Dr Sillery told me all about you when we talked on the phone last week. I do hope you're going to show us what you crazy Cretans do for a good time while we're here.'

Anna gazed into her coffee while Miranda simpered. So she had known about Vangelis before they even got on the plane? That wasn't such a surprise. Anna thought ungenerously for a moment that Miranda had kept his presence quiet so that she could get a head start in the beauty stakes because she thought she needed one. Then Anna cut the thought dead. After all, what did it matter? Even if she didn't have Justin back in London, Anna was in Crete to work.

Anyway, Vangelis's attention had been completely monopolised by the beautiful blonde girl who had appeared at his side. Miranda ran her slender fingers through his curly thick hair, lamenting that the best locks are always wasted on men. Vangelis contradicted her, saying that he had never seen such wonderful golden tresses as hers. Anna, feeling her pale Saxon shoulders reddening in the sun already, sank back into the shade of the house and sipped her coffee thoughtfully, until at last they were joined by Dr Sillery, or the Fuhrer, as he was sometimes known – but not to his face of course.

'Can't you do something with that bloody

cockerel of yours, Vangelis? Like make him guest of honour at Sunday dinner?' Dr Sillery grumbled as he pulled up a chair and sniffed disdainfully at the hard cold toast. The girls and Vangelis had already polished off the yogurt.

Miranda and Anna straightened up in their seats like two naughty schoolgirls. William Sillery had yet to acknowledge their presence. They watched silently as the tall thin man began to butter a slice of the cold toast in the absence of anything better, before devouring it in just three large bites.

William Sillery wasn't supposed to look like this, Anna thought. Everyone who had worked with him had described him as a slightly podgy man, given to going red even in the shade. Now, here he was, lean and mean-looking as you like, with his smooth skin toasty-brown like perfect caramel. Anna was amazed to find that she might even have rated him a six out of ten on her scale of attractiveness. Miranda's open mouth betrayed the fact that she was having similar thoughts.

'Uh-hmm, Dr Sillery,' Miranda cleared her throat.

'Have you had the pleasure of being introduced to Anna Hazel?' Anna extended her hand nervously.

'Great to meet you in person at last.'

'You, too,' said William Sillery, allowing just a flicker of a smile to reach his lips. 'Glad to see you made it out here safely at last. Hope you're ready to start work.'

'Yes. Of course I am,' Anna said keenly.

'Good, because thanks to your flight delay last night we've lost a lot of time already. I want to get cracking straight after breakfast.'

'Straight after breakfast? But it's Sunday,' Miranda protested weakly 'I thought we might have an hour or two to get acclimatised at least.'

Or rather, to get acquainted with Vangelis, thought Anna.

'We have just two months before our precious site is bulldozed to pieces for a bloody great hotel, Ms Sharpe. If you wanted to get acclimatised to Crete, you should have come here with Thomas Cook.'

Feeling thoroughly told off, the girls retreated

from the breakfast table to get kitted out in their digging gear. Anna slavered herself with factor fifty sunscreen and wore a T-shirt with a collar that she could turn up if she had to. When she met up with Miranda in the lobby however, she was surprised to see that the other girl was wearing shorts designed for someone much smaller, and a halter-neck top that just about protected her nipples.

'Are you going to be OK in that get-up?' Anna asked. 'The sun's pretty strong out there, you know.'

'That bastard Sillery may think he has rights to my Sunday morning but he is not going to stop me from getting a tan,' Miranda replied tetchily. 'Besides, if I do start to feel sunburnt, I shall just have to come back inside and have Vangelis apply calamine lotion to every part of my body.'

Anna smiled. 'That doesn't sound like such a bad idea.'

When Dr Sillery was ready, the workers piled into an ancient jeep driven by Vangelis and drove up to the site. At first sight, it looked pretty much like every other barren, dusty field they passed, but as they drew nearer, Anna could see that it had already been marked out in a grid with long pieces of string and that a top layer of the soil had been removed by a digger. What was to follow was weeks of gently scraping away another layer on hands and knees, logging everything they found with photographs and section diagrams. Anna gulped at the enormity of the site. And there were really only four of them to deal with it?

Dr Sillery handed out the instruments and set everyone to work. Miranda wielded her trowel as though she were about to pull an irritating little weed out of a Home Counties garden. Vangelis sprang gracefully down into a hole he had made earlier and set to work with more enthusiasm than Anna had ever before seen for what appeared to be nothing but a field of dry dirt.

By that evening, at the end of a fairly unfruitful day, Anna really needed to sleep. Her back ached, her knees ached and her shoulders were stinging like crazy where they had been burned by the relentless Cretan sun even through her thick cotton

T-shirt. But Dr Sillery had no time for softies, and he kept everyone up way into the early hours, sitting around the kitchen table on uncomfortable stools, while he explained what he hoped to find in his patch of unpromising ground.

'I chose you people to work with me because you are rumoured to be the best in your field,' he said, clenching his fist in a gesture designed to pep them up. Anna smiled. Miranda yawned.

Finally, he bid them goodnight, after setting a ridiculously early breakfast time, and retired to his room. But Vangelis, Anna and Miranda continued to sit around the kitchen table staring at the plans Sillery had scribbled out as if they would never be able to move again.

'He is such a shit,' said Miranda finally. 'I ache all over.'

'He's just worried that we don't have much time to work here,' Vangelis countered reasonably.

'Well, if this is how he's going to be for the next two months, I might just have to teach him a lesson about being nice to his employees.'

'How will you do that?' Vangelis asked.

'I don't know what I'm going to do about it right now,' Miranda continued. 'But I'll think of something spectacular before the end of this dig. Just you wait and see.'

Anna didn't want to stay up and plot. She was tired and more than a little sad after another day without news from Justin. There was a faint signal up at the site of the dig, but no messages had come through except a text from her mother and another one reminding her it would cost a king's ransom to use her phone overseas. So Anna made her excuses and went upstairs to lie on her hard bed. However, as soon as she left the kitchen, she heard the scraping of a chair across marble as Miranda drew herself closer to Vangelis. This was followed by a prolonged bout of whispering and giggling. Anna wondered how Miranda had the energy to flirt at this time of night. Later she admitted to herself that perhaps she was secretly disappointed that the only man in the vicinity worth fantasising about was already very much under siege.

Chapter Four

Risking the wrath of the little things that bite in the night, Anna opened her window to let a breeze into her still-aired room. Though she had been in bed for more than an hour, she could hear that Vangelis and Miranda were still up and talking quietly. The back door creaked open and they stepped out into the garden not far from Anna's window. She heard another soft giggle. A stifled moan.

Anna rose slowly from her bed. There was no way she would be able to sleep while she could still hear Miranda's unsubtle attempts at seduction. She walked to the window intending to close it against the distraction, but as she did so, the breeze shifted the curtains so that she could see the two figures of her colleagues clearly silhouetted by moonlight outside.

They were standing together at the very edge of the garden, looking down across the cliff to the sea. Miranda had one slender hand on Vangelis's rugged shoulder. Her head was tipped coquettishly to one side as she laughed at some joke. With her free hand, Miranda pushed back her beautiful golden hair, which was now hanging loose about her shoulders like a veil. Vangelis turned towards her and she moved almost imperceptibly closer to him, standing on tiptoe until her pelvis touched the intricate silver buckle of his belt.

Unable to stop herself, Anna held back the slightly open curtain, mesmerised by the scene of seduction outside. Already she had done it. Already Miranda had a new man to take her mind off the one she had left behind. As Anna watched, her bubbly blonde colleague rose up to shorten even further the gap between their softly murmuring lips. Simultaneously

Vangelis inclined his head towards hers, then Miranda took her head in his hands and pulled him closer still.

Their lips met.

And Anna felt a stab of pain. It was envy, of course. But not envy because Miranda had captured the delectable Vangelis. Rather it was envy that they were sharing the beautiful moonlight together while Anna could only watch the moon's slow passage across the sky alone. How nice it would have been to share the view with Justin. She let the curtain fall closed again and retreated to her bed without closing the window. The noise it made in shutting would make it obvious that she had seen it all.

Anna lay down on the hard cool bed and gazed at the brass and wooden fan that hung from the ceiling. Soon, she was remembering a time when she had been kissed in the moonlight. A time when she had held a lover's hand tightly as together they watched the dark sea mysteriously churning up the secrets it held in its depths.

It had been just a year ago, when she and Justin were holidaying in Thailand. Anna had saved up for ages to match Justin's spending power on a holiday that he could have paid off in a week. But it was worth it. Away from the City for three whole weeks that time, Justin had been at his very best. They had found themselves a small hotel that nestled in a clump of palm trees right on the edge of the golden beach. They had a stark white painted room, with a fan on the ceiling not unlike the one that Anna gazed at now.

At midday, when the sun got too hot, they would go inside for a siesta. Except that they never did get any sleep. Instead, they would take a long slow shower to wash the salt-water of a morning's swimming from their bodies. Justin would soap her down first and then she would do the same for him. By the time she reached his penis, he was always already hard but she would lather her hands up anyway, making a big show of washing him clean as the thick shaft of his penis throbbed hotly in her palm. Once, he grew so impatient to rinse off and take her back to the wide double bed in the other room that he pushed her against the cold tiled wall of the shower cubicle and forced himself into her there and then. She had to wrap one long brown leg around him and cling like crazy to the slippery surface of the wall to stop herself from falling over.

The warm water pounded down on them, running between their faces and into their mouths as they kissed like hungry cannibals. Unable to get the friction he needed to truly take her on the shower floor, Justin had lifted her out of there, with his penis still deep inside her, and carried her across to the sink with her legs wrapped tight around his waist. There, he had placed her carefully on the floor and turned her around, and when she had both hands on the basin to steady her, he had entered her from behind with a force and a passion she had never felt before. His hands grabbed for her swollen breasts as she leaned forward, barely able to hang on to the slippery porcelain in her excitement. As she sensed him nearing his climax, she forced her head up to look into the mirror, knowing that the sight of his face in ecstasy would push her even nearer to her own.

Anna's legs shuddered as Justin powered into her. Each time he moved it was as though his penis grew a little longer, a little harder, until his final thrust seemed to fill her whole body with heat.

'Anna,' he cried out in ecstatic anguish as the semen shot from his marble-hard shaft.

She threw herself backwards against him and tried to cling on to his thighs with her hands. His pelvis jerked frantically against her buttocks as though powered by erotic electricity, and then suddenly she knew she was coming too, feeling the juice of her pent-up desire flooding down her vagina towards him, until it mingled with the water from the shower on her thighs.

Her waking dream finished, Anna couldn't help listening out again for the sound of Miranda and Vangelis outside. But all was silent again now. She could hear nothing but the night calls of the crickets and the constant lament of the restless sea as it stroked the silent shore like an unrequited lover. Anna squinted at the screen of her useless phone in the darkness. It was almost two o'clock in the morning. In less than four hours, Georgios the cock would be telling her that it was time to get up again.

Chapter Five

At breakfast, Miranda looked a wreck. Two sleepless nights in a row had obviously caught up with her, and not even her budding tan could disguise the big dark circles under her eyes.

'Sleep well?' Dr Sillery asked with more than a hint of sarcasm.

Miranda shared a secret look with Anna across the table that suggested the reason why she hadn't.

'I'm sure I'll get used to it, Dr Sillery,' Miranda sighed to him. 'It's just that these Cretan beds really are terribly hard.'

'That's because they're made on stone bases so that you can't push them together,' said Vangelis cheekily; and Anna was surprised when Miranda shot him a look that didn't suggest complicity so much as 'Why don't you just shut up?'

'Yes. Well, you'll have to get to bed earlier in the future,' Dr Sillery continued, without appearing to notice the conversation's angry undercurrent. 'This isn't Cyprus and I don't want you falling asleep on this job, Ms Sharpe.'

Miranda didn't reply, but got to her feet and excused herself to the bathroom. Dr Sillery suggested the presence of premenstrual tension as a reason for her sudden disappearance. Vangelis, not quite understanding the reference, shrugged in agreement.

Anna felt momentarily sorry for Miranda, but only momentarily. After all, she hadn't been forced to stay up all night with Vangelis on only their second night in Crete. She could have had all the 'Z's' she wanted instead. But on the way to the dig, Anna was careful to keep the meaningless banter to a minimum anyway.

'So, tell me more about your love life,' Miranda said suddenly.

Anna looked up in surprise from the area of sand she was carefully brushing away. If Miranda talked at all that morning, Anna had expected that it would be about her own moonlit adventures with Vangelis.

'You said you had to leave someone behind to come out here. Why don't you tell me about him? Had you been going out long?'

'Six years.'

'That's long,' Miranda sighed.

'Yeah. I suppose it is.' Anna sat back on her haunches to get a better look at something that might have been a piece of painted tile.

'Tell me more,' Miranda interrupted.

Anna put the shard of tile down again. 'OK. His name is Justin. He's tall and blond. Wears glasses sometimes – though not when we're out clubbing because he's so vain,' she added with a laugh. 'We met at university. He was studying archaeology too. Same year, different college. But now he works in the City. He's a broker for one of the big foreign banks.'

Miranda sat back on her heels too and perked up when she heard what Justin did. 'Banking, eh? Is the sex better now that he's working in the City?'

'Well,' Anna laughed with surprise. 'Since you ask, yes, I suppose it is. But I think it might be that we just know each other better now, rather than his job having made the difference.'

'Don't you believe it,' Miranda replied. 'I'm a firm believer in the idea that money and power are the best known aphrodisiacs. In this profession there's no money at all. That's why male archaeologists are always such a wash-out when it comes to the sack.' She said this last comment slightly more loudly than the rest. From the corner of her eye, Anna was sure she noticed Vangelis lift his head to listen.

'Yeah,' Miranda elaborated. 'In fact, you could apply my findings to academics in general. I only got into this bloody digging business because I thought it would be a great way to meet sensitive intellectual men. But they're not sensitive at all. Just timid. They never make the first move. It takes them months and months of fannying about before they even pluck up the courage to give you a kiss on the lips. And then, when you finally get them into bed, they inevitably want you to dress up like a school-girl or, worst of all, pretend to be their mummy.'

Vangelis was definitely listening now.

'But when a man has money and real power, it gives him confidence. And confidence in bed is everything. Second to really enjoying what he's doing, of course. Most archaeologists are more excited about finding a Roman mosaic depicting a sexual act than actually getting down to it and doing the act themselves.' Miranda was jabbing at the earth in front of her to emphasise her point. 'They don't recognise the beauty of a real living, breathing woman. An archaeologist would get more aroused if he had just dug you up from a peat bog only partially preserved.'

'Miranda,' Dr Sillery called from a carefully delineated square a few feet away. 'Will you be a bit more careful about where you're putting that trowel? There might be something truly wonderful under there and you could be smashing it to bits with your cack-handedness.'

'See, that's all that matters to them. Some bloody Minoan pot.' Miranda flung her trowel down on the earth and stormed off in the direction of the tent where the things they had already found were laid out and catalogued.

'What's wrong with her?' asked Vangelis, as his eyes crinkled up in a beautiful smile.

'Oh, nothing,' said Anna. Though she suspected that the correct answer would have been: 'you'.

Indeed, that night at dinner, Miranda and Vangelis barely shared a word. Fortunately, Dr Sillery was only too happy to keep the conversation afloat by holding forth with his theories. He was convinced that beneath the site they were working on lay a palace that could easily turn out to be as big as the famous labyrinth at Knossos. They had already hit the remains of several walls which still bore the faintest traces of bright painted murals of palace life. Shards of pottery were turning up in every other spadeful now. Dr Sillery was in his element.

'See? It's unnatural,' Miranda complained in a whisper to Anna again. 'The way these guys get so bloody excited about pots.'

Anna nodded sagely. Though if the truth be told, she herself was pretty excited about the pots they hoped to find. It had long been her dream to be part of a team that stumbled across a potentially history-changing site, like Tutankhamun's tomb or Knossos. Later that night, she walked half an hour from the house to find a flicker of signal and tried to call Justin, eager to tell him what had already been found. She had decided that the best way to tackle their last heated conversation was to pretend it hadn't happened. Even taking the time difference into consideration, she knew she would be catching him at ten o'clock at night. But there was no answer. Feeling hurt, she didn't bother to leave a message. It was Monday night. Surely he wouldn't have gone out? And it was too early for him to be in bed. Left to his own devices, Justin would have been nocturnal. Perhaps he was still at work, she told herself. Towards the end of the month, when a whole rack of figures had to be presented to the boss, things often got hectic for Justin.

By the time she gave up on the phone, everyone else had already gone to bed. Anna followed suit, but she couldn't seem to sleep even though there was no disturbance from Miranda and Vangelis that night. Her head was full of Justin. He must be screening his calls, ignoring and avoiding her. She knew they had parted on bad terms, but had they really said goodbye for the last time?

Anna was so deep in thought that she barely heard the knock at her door.

'Anna, are you asleep yet?'

She didn't answer first time. The knock came again.

'Anna, it's me. Open up, will you?'

'Who's "me"?' Anna asked cautiously.

'Me,' said the visitor as she pushed open the

door. It was Miranda, dressed no longer in her pyjamas but up to the nines in a blue stretch dress made for someone much smaller in several crucial areas.

'Coming out?' she whispered.

'You have got to be joking,' replied Anna. 'Don't you know what time it is?'

'Sure, I do. It's two-thirty in the morning. But this isn't London, you know. The one good thing about this wretched, godforsaken dump of an island is that they don't have such stupid licensing hours.'

'I think I'll see you in the morning,' Anna muttered, getting back into bed and turning her face into her pillow as she tried to ignore Miranda's pleas.

'Oh, come on, Anna. It's been so boring since we got here,' Miranda sighed.

'We've only been here for three days,' groaned Anna.

'Exactly. Three days too long. Listen, apparently there's a village just down the road with a pretty decent-sized taverna. It's bound to be open. I just want to feel like I'm living in the modern world again. Hear some funky music. Have a little dance.'

She gave a demonstrative shimmy.

'It'll all be bouzouki music,' Anna protested.

'I don't care what it is, as long as it's not Sillery's bloody Vivaldi.'

'I'm not coming with you.'

But Miranda wasn't going to take no for an answer. Pretty soon, she had physically dragged Anna out of her bed and was pulling things out of her suitcase that might be suitable for a night on the town.

'Christ, Anna. Have you got nothing with you but tatty old jeans and T-shirts?'

'I didn't think I'd need a ball gown for this trip.'

'A girl can always find the need for a ball gown,' said Miranda wisely.

'Where you come from, perhaps . . .'

'You've just got to make your opportunities.'

'For what?'

'For meeting a millionaire who's just moored his yacht in the harbour,' Miranda said dreamily.

'It's a fishing village.'

'So was Cannes.'

Miranda wasn't about to give up, though in the end, she decided that she was going to have to lend Anna something of hers before the country girl would look respectable. The garment in question was a stretchy little dress made from red Lycra that probably looked great with Miranda's hair, though Anna wasn't so sure how it went with hers. Miranda tried to lend her some of her strappy shoes as well, but Anna flatly refused, saying that she did not want to risk a broken ankle on the rough path down to the village.

'That dress does not look right with Birkenstocks,' Miranda persisted when Anna said that she was ready.

Anna replied, 'This dress does not look right with me. If you want me to come with you at all, I'm afraid that you'll just have to live with the shoes.'

Miranda bit her lip. 'I guess you've got me over a barrel on this one.'

So they set off – Miranda in a pair of

ankle-threatening strappy blue wedges and Anna in her sensible old Birkenstocks. A dark and dangerous half hour on the rocky footpath to the village later, the girls walked into the taverna. As they entered, the little room fell silent. There were hardly any women in there amongst the Greek men playing endless games of backgammon and smoking vile cigars, and they were certainly not wearing dresses that might have been mistaken for swimsuits.

Anna clung to Miranda's arm. 'This is just like that scene in *An American Werewolf in London*,' she complained. 'Let's get out of here before something terrible happens.'

For a moment, it seemed as though even the brave and brazen Miranda might have been forced to reconsider their plans but then, as suddenly as it had stopped, the bouzouki music resumed and the leering eyes returned to the backgammon boards. The proprietor of the taverna, who was drying glasses behind the bar, waved an arm expansively to direct the girls to an empty table in a dark corner by the door. Miranda seemed disappointed, but Anna was relieved that their little alcove was almost private. When they were seated, the barman came out to them instantly with two small shot glasses filled with a thick liquid that smelled ominously of paint stripper. An aperitif, the girls supposed – though perhaps it was for taking off their nail varnish. 'Yamas,' said the barman, as he put the glasses down.

'I think that means "cheers" in Greek,' said Miranda helpfully. She picked up her glass and knocked it straight back while the barman watched. 'Yamas! Urgh, that's vile.'

'You can have mine then,' said Anna.

'OK. I will.' Miranda finished off Anna's share as well. 'What else do you want?'

'Beer, I guess. That can't taste too different from the stuff back home, can it?'

Nodding sagely, the barman obliged. But this time, when he set down the glasses, he set himself down beside them as well. Anna smiled nervously at the man who had joined them, but she needn't have worried about perfecting a friendly expression because the barman's attention had been fully on Miranda's cleavage from the moment she arrived. Miranda obligingly flicked back her huge mane of golden hair to give him a better view. She told Anna that she was used to people talking to her breasts rather than her brain. Sometimes she even quite liked it. It gave her a feeling of feminine power.

'You are both English ladies, yes?' he asked, without lifting his gaze for one second. Anna was struck by the whiteness of the barman's teeth against his tanned skin as he smiled at her friend's perfect orbs.

'I'm Scottish, actually,' Miranda corrected him primly.

'English. Scottish. It is all the same to me.'

'Like Greek and Turkish Cypriot?' Miranda retorted. The barman looked unimpressed. Anna smiled desperately, praying that she wasn't about to become caught up in a political row.

'I have learned English for many years,' the barman continued regardless, signifying to Anna's relief that he wasn't about to debate national differences. 'My name is Nicky.' Miranda oblig-ingly introduced Anna and herself. 'I want eventu-ally to come to England for a holiday myself.'

'Oh, really. I must to give you my address,' said Miranda sarcastically.

'That would be very kind of you. I will call you when I am going to come and let you know how long I need to stay.'

Anna rolled her eyes. What was Miranda getting them into?

'You are a very beautiful lady.' Nicky placed a hand on Miranda's knee and she swiftly removed it for him. 'Your hair is like the bright shining sun reflected on the sea.' He put his hand on her knee again and this time she let it stay there. Obviously playing hard to get had become too hard to be bothered with. 'I have a friend here,' Nicky contin-ued insistently. 'His name is Phil and he has a boat in the harbour. When the taverna is closed, perhaps we can go out on the sea together and watch the sun come up over the island?'

Miranda looked to Anna for an answer, her eyes

smiling at the possibility. Anna hoped her own eyes screamed, 'No, no, no,' since it sounded like the kind of invitation that she most certainly wanted to refuse. But Nicky continued to lay on the cheesy metaphors, and before long Anna knew that Miranda was hooked. She was going to go out to sea regardless of whether Anna wanted to join them or not. In the end, Anna decided that she better had go along too, just in case. It wouldn't do to leave Miranda alone at sea with two strangers.

But Miranda got by far the better deal. Nicky at least had all his parts in the right place and you wouldn't have thrown him out of bed for farting. In fact, his tight white shirt hinted at a pretty good body beneath, and when he smiled his forty-watt smile you could almost call him handsome. The famous Phil, however, was a good foot shorter than Anna and he was slightly cross-eyed, like a teacher at Anna's old school. Miss Hargreave had put the fear of God into all her pupils since none of them could tell whether it was them, or the person next to them, who was being ticked off in her class. It was like that with Phil. He had talked about his boat for a good half an hour before Anna realised that he was actually addressing her and though she wasn't exactly enthralled by the idea of the trip, she didn't want to appear snooty to their host. Perhaps, she thought later, as he tried to put his arm round her on the way down to the jetty, it would be best if she didn't overcompensate.

Once they were far out enough in the bay for the lights of the village to look just as big as the twinkling stars above them, Nicky, who had been playing captain, stopped the engine of the boat and dropped the anchor.

'We will stay here and admire the view for a while,' he announced. But without a second glance at the scenery, Miranda skipped straight from the prow of the boat to follow him into the tiny dark cabin. Anna remained stranded on the deck with Phil, feeling slightly sick from more than just the rocking of the boat.

'It is beautiful, yes?' he asked her.

Anna nodded. However awkward the situation was, there could be no doubt that the view was beautiful. It was as if someone had thrown a string of fairy lights around the island.

'Beautiful like you,' Phil continued.

Anna blushed and concentrated on the view.

'That's very kind of you,' she muttered.

'Not kind,' he said, taking her chin in his hand. 'I think that I am the lucky one to be here tonight with you.' Anna took his hand away from her chin and smiled stiffly. Miranda was really going to owe her for this one. Miles out to sea with two guys they hardly knew, and Anna was stuck with the ugly one she had no intention of getting to know better.

'Your hair is like shoe polish,' he said, not altogether successfully, as he lifted a thick strand of Anna's light brown hair and let it trail over his fingers.

'Shoe polish?' she repeated.

'Shiny.'

'Thanks.' She had heard worse. But not by much.

'Can I kiss you?' he asked then.

Anna shook her head in horror. 'No. No, you can't,' she squeaked.

'Is there someone else?' Phil asked sincerely, as though that was the only possible reason for her refusal to bump lips with him. 'Someone you left behind in England?'

Anna nodded quickly.

'I understand,' said Phil, and for a moment it seemed as though he might stop his badgering. Though whether there was someone in England for Anna any more she was no longer really sure.

Miranda had no such qualms about getting to know Nicky the barman. He had barely shut the cabin door behind them before she was helping him take his dirty white shirt off over his head, revealing his thick brown chest beneath. She wasn't disappointed. She ran her hands feverishly over his tight muscles, twisting her fingers in the hair that smattered his chest between his pecs, as though she hadn't had sex in years. (Well, it had been at least a week.) She almost growled with anticipation as

Nick took hold of the hem of her flimsy skirt and began to edge it upwards over her hips.

'You are so gorgeous,' he hissed in her ear, pronouncing it 'george-eous'.

'I know,' she replied, as she lifted her arms to help him pull her dress off. She had been wearing nothing but her perfume underneath. When Nicky looked surprised by her nakedness, she told him simply, 'It's hot out here,' and then continued to strike poses for his approval in the semi-darkness.

Miranda Sharpe knew that she had everything to show off about. Her generous round breasts were accentuated by a hand-span waist and neatly proportioned hips that flowed seamlessly into long, long legs. Her skin, she knew, was as smooth and even coloured as the skin of an almost ripe peach. And so it should be, she thought, since she had spent plenty of time slathering on potions to look after it – especially over the last few days, repairing the damage done by having to work in the blistering sun from dawn to dusk.

Nicky reached out a hand to touch her hesitantly, as though she were a statue that at any moment might spring into life and surprise him.

'Are you just going to stand there and look at me?' she asked him provocatively.

No, he was not. He took his shaking fingers away from her shoulder instantly and began to fumble with his thick leather belt. His face was a mask of frustration as the buckle evaded him for a few seconds; then, with the buckle finally free, he pushed his trousers down over his knees at such speed you might have thought they were made of some acid-coated material that was stripping the skin from his thighs. Miranda crouched down and helped him unlace his shoes, which he kicked off in the direction of an untidy pile of life-jackets. Then she helped him pull his trousers off over his feet while he simultaneously pushed down his pants like a man in a race to get undressed.

Miranda shrieked with delight as his penis sprang free and smacked her square in the middle of the forehead while she was still freeing his feet from his sandals.

'Naughty boy,' she laughed, taking hold of the satisfyingly broad shaft in her right hand and sticking it straight into her mouth like a lollipop.

'Ohmigod,' Nicky moaned, as she started to lick him into shape. 'Oh . . . my . . .' He hadn't even kissed her yet.

'There. That's much better, isn't it?' Miranda briefly took her mouth away from his crotch and surveyed her handiwork. Even in the darkness of the boat's cabin, she could see that she had landed herself a prime catch. Nicky stumbled backwards until he landed on the captain's seat, where he sat catching his breath and staring at this incredible English girl in amazement.

Licking her lips, Miranda stepped forward and stood astride his knees. Drawing a finger tantalisingly slowly down the centre of his body, she sighed as she contemplated what to do next. Nicky breathed heavily, his cock rising and falling in time with his chest. Miranda moved closer so that her pussy hovered mere millimetres above his proud member, tempting him upwards and into her. Then she sat down carefully on the tops of his thighs, so that his dick stood up between them in such a way that it might have been his or hers if you weren't looking closely enough.

Miranda lunged forward and began to kiss him, covering his soft, generous lips with her hungry mouth. Nicky clutched her body against him as his tongue probed deep inside her. Between them, his penis twitched as it grew ever harder. Miranda loved the silky feel of the warmly throbbing shaft against her belly as she ground her body against his. His dick reached up as far as her belly button and she couldn't wait for it to reach that far on the inside.

Pulling her mouth away from his, she leaned back a little and took hold of his penis, working the tight foreskin backwards and forwards until Nicky thought he might explode. He placed a hand on each of her full breasts and kneaded them passionately until her nipples stood out and begged to be kissed. Miranda gasped as he took one swollen nipple into his mouth and sucked at it, hard. The thrill of the sensation teetering on the edge between pleasure and pain made her grasp his penis ever more firmly and slick that foreskin ever more quickly.

'Oh, I can't stand this much longer,' she breathed excitedly. Though he had yet to touch her there, her pussy was so wet, she was sure that he must be able to feel her love-juice dripping out of her body and on to his leg. 'I need you inside me, Nicky,' she whispered to him. She raised herself up from his thighs and moved forwards again to position herself once more above his throbbing shaft.

Nicky closed his eyes tightly as he waited for her to take hold of his penis and put it inside her aching vagina. She wrapped her arms around his nut-brown neck and eased her body upwards so that the very tip of his dick was pointing at the entrance to her desire. She rocked slowly back and forth, undulating across him so that the pinky head of his glans dragged teasingly over her smooth flesh. She was so wet with longing for him. She could almost taste her desire on the still air in that cabin. Nicky shivered as she drew her fingernails down the side of his neck.

Impatiently Nicky took hold of his penis himself and carefully began to guide it inside her. Miranda complied, easing herself down inch by glorious inch, until she felt Nicky's balls make delicious contact with her gently rounded bottom. Her hands on his thickly muscled neck told her that he was already flushing hotly with this unexpected answering of his most heartfelt wishes.

Miranda braced her feet, which were still in their high strappy shoes, against the hard floor of the cabin so that she could move herself up and down Nicky's slippery shaft by merely bending and then straightening out her knees. Her arms were still wrapped around his neck. She looked deep into his liquid brown eyes, which glittered with the moonlight reflected off the ocean outside. She wondered if her own green eyes looked the same. Gorgeous. They usually did. Her lower lip trembled delicately as she oozed up and down his shaft with tantalising precision.

'Don't move,' she told him when she had begun to gather speed and he tried to alter the pace by making movements of his own. 'I'm in charge here.' With each downward stroke, she hesitated for a moment and tightened her vaginal muscles around him as hard as she could. He seemed to be enjoying it, for each skilful squeeze elicited a shuddering sigh from his lips. His eyes were tightly closed against reality.

Then suddenly, Nicky tried to get up. He reached blindly behind his chair, looking for a blanket to throw on to the wooden floor of the cabin before he pushed Miranda down on to it. From being so perfectly in control, Miranda found that she was suddenly no longer the one on top. With her lying beneath him at last on the floor of the boat, Nicky began to force his way into her frantically. There was no real rhythm to his movements now. He was totally controlled by the power of his desire. Frantic. Frenzied. Like an animal.

Pinned beneath him, Miranda could hardly move at all and yet her whole body was buzzing, shivering, writhing inside. She shrieked with surprise as he grasped one of her thighs and pulled her shaking leg up towards her chest. He was powering into her from an angle now and she felt utterly, utterly open to him. She was so wet with desire that the juice of her longing for him was already running down the inside of her trembling thigh.

'Nicky, Nicky, stop, stop, stop!' she squealed, though the ecstatic laughter in her voice and the insistence of her hands driving his buttocks towards her again and again and again told him that that was not what she actually meant this time. Miranda felt as though every drop of blood in her body was rushing towards her vagina now. Her head was becoming light, giddy, dizzy with the sensation of delight growing inside her. Out of the darkness of the cabin, bright flashes of every colour swam before her eyes like incredible firework explosions generated by the heat between their shuddering bodies.

Nicky, too, felt his entire body begin to harden towards his goal. He was just seconds away from his climax now. His balls were aching to be free of their hot spermy load. He longed to shoot jets of creamy white jism deep inside her and hear her beg for more.

'Aaaah, aaaah, Miranda,' he moaned dramatically. Then his body reared up and he twisted away from her as he began to climax violently. His face contorted into a mask of agonised ecstasy. His teeth were bared, gritted together, glittering in the dark.

The thick white cum thundered through his penis to explode into Miranda's body with the force of a well-aimed missile. Beneath him she still thrashed about like a serpent on the filthy grey blanket. Her own pleasure was splitting her in half as it raced from her vagina to her head and back again. Her pelvis rose automatically to meet his downward thrusts. Then she wrapped her legs tightly around his back, holding them pressed hard together, pulling him in.

'Aaieee!!' Nicky shouted suddenly as the last of his cum tore from his groin like a bullet and Miranda pressed herself hard against him as if her life depended on her ability to melt herself into his flesh.

But her own body was calming down already. The violent early spasms of her orgasm were fading to a distant tremble.

When he had finished, Miranda still clasped Nicky's exhausted body to her own. She drew her fingers across his back, still slick and wet with sweat, stroking him down into calmness until she began to become aware of the outside world again, and, in particular, the softly murmuring voices of her colleague Anna, and Nicky's friend Phil on the deck outside.

Chapter Six

'Have a good time?' Anna asked rhetorically as they climbed slowly back up the steep hill to the villa.

'Yes, thank you. I did.'

'Not that I actually needed to ask,' Anna added. 'You guys were shaking the boat so much I thought that Phil and I were going to be thrown overboard and drowned.'

'That is an exaggeration.'

'I put on a life-jacket.'

At that, Miranda looked faintly pleased with herself. It had been quite an epic performance, hadn't it, she thought. 'Anyway, what are you looking so sour-faced about, Anna Hazel?' she laughed. 'I didn't leave you on your own, did I? What happened with funky Phil the fisherman?'

'Nothing.'

'Nothing? Is that absolutely nothing? Or just nothing worth shouting about?'

'Absolutely nothing, thank you very much!' Anna exclaimed indignantly. 'It is possible for a girl to spend time with a man and still feel disinclined to jump him, you know. Especially if he looks like he's a bit player from a horror film.'

'I guess he was a bit of a dog.'

'A bit of a dog? That's the understatement of the year. He made Quasimodo look like a master of deportment. And those eyes. One on my fanny and one on my tits. That was really spooky. Besides, I've got someone at home. Remember?'

'Well, you can forget him,' said Miranda flatly. 'From what you've told me about your man so far, by the time you get back to England, it will be well and truly over between you and Justin. You should get yourself some local action while you can. If fisherman Phil's not up to your exacting standards, what about Vangelis? He seems to be very fond of you.'

'Really?'

'I've seen him giving you the glad eye when you bend over to pick up a pot.'

Anna wasn't sure whether Miranda was spoiling for a fight so she didn't bother to press further. Instead, she shrugged her shoulders and said, 'Men, schmen.' Though once she was inside again, getting undressed for bed, she realised that she actually felt faintly flattered by Miranda's observation. Vangelis was certainly a damn sight nearer Anna's idea of a Greek god than Phil.

In the morning however, Vangelis wasn't his usual friendly self. Anna woke late. When she looked at the watch on her bedside table and saw that she had overslept by almost an hour, she jumped out of bed with such speed that she nearly broke her neck sliding across the marble floor on her way to the bathroom.

In the kitchen, Vangelis was scraping the remains of his breakfast into the dustbin with a displeased look on his handsome face. Miranda was nowhere to be seen.

'Dr Sillery has already gone to the site,' Vangelis said flatly, without even wishing Anna good morning.

'And Miranda? Has she gone up there too?' Anna asked. It would be typical of that sneaky cow to have got up early, despite keeping her out all night, and not to have given Anna a wake-up call on her way down to breakfast.

'No,' said Vangelis. 'I do not think she is awake yet.'

'Oh.'

Anna poured herself a cup of coffee and took her place opposite him at the table, already feeling slightly on edge.

'You went out last night after we went to bed?' Vangelis asked.

'Er . . . yes,' replied Anna, feeling strangely guilty under Vangelis's gaze. 'Couldn't sleep.'

'You went to the taverna?'

'We did. It's quite nice in there, isn't it? Friendly people. Really nice.'

'But you didn't come home when it closed for the night,' Vangelis continued. 'I saw you down by the harbour. You and your friend Miranda.'

'You did?'

'Yes. I couldn't sleep either. So I thought I would go for a walk by the sea. And I saw you down by the harbour with your friends Nicky and Phil from the taverna. Did they take you for a special ride on their boat, by any chance?'

Anna cast her eyes down to the tablecloth, still not really knowing why she felt so twitchy. 'We went for a little ride in Phil's boat, yes,' she said, as nonchalantly as she could. 'We wanted to see what the village looks like from the sea.'

Vangelis snorted. 'Very nice. You know what they call that boat, Anna?'

'Can't say I asked them. Some sort of girl's name, I suppose?'

'Anna, they call that boat the *Ship of Whores*.'

'I'm sorry?' Anna wasn't sure she had heard him right.

'The *Ship of Whores*,' Vangelis repeated more slowly, as if he were saying something for the benefit of the very stupid. 'Every foreign girl who passes through this little town gets an invitation for a ride around the bay on that boat.'

'Is that so?' said Anna, as she bit a piece of toast.

'Yes it is. And your lovely, gentle hosts, Nicky and Phil, have a big list of the girls they invited on the back of the door in the taverna kitchen. Every time a girl goes for a sail with them, they write her name on the back of the door and give her points out of ten for her performance.'

Anna could feel the blood draining from her cheeks as the toast turned to ash in her mouth. She could almost see her name written neatly on Phil's side of the page, even though she knew she hadn't actually put in any kind of performance at all.

'I have to say that I thought you would be more careful than the others, Anna. I didn't think that you were the kind of girl whose head could be turned by a few flattering words.'

'I'm not – it wasn't,' Anna began to protest. But Vangelis was already on his feet and heading for the door. He passed Miranda on the way out, without bothering to say hello. She took his place at the table and looked in surprise at Anna's pale face.

'Feeling all right, Anna? You look terrible. What's up?'

'You don't want to know.'

'I always want to know,' said Miranda.

Anna took a deep breath and began to tell her story. 'I just had a bit of a weird conversation with Vangelis, that's all. He saw us going out on the boat last night. He says he knows Nicky and Phil quite well. He knows their boat well, too. Apparently, it's called the *Ship of Whores,* and all the foreign girls the men lure out on it have their names written up on a big list in the kitchen at the taverna – with scores.'

'Scores?' asked Miranda, her eyes widening to the size of saucers.

'Yes, scores. For performance. Out of ten. Oh, God, Miranda. I feel sick just thinking about it. So used.'

But Miranda seemed unfazed. She took a big bite out of a piece of toast and said with her mouth full, 'Scores out of ten, eh? Well, I'm not worried about that, since I know I played a blinder last night. By the time I had finished with him, that Nicky boy was shaking like a leaf. And I can't say I know what you're worried about either. You told me that Phil had nothing to mark you on anyway. Or does he?'

'No, he does not,' Anna retorted. 'How desperate do you think I am? But, I still can't help feeling used by that bastard. I'm so embarrassed.'

'What on earth are you embarrassed for?' Miranda sighed. 'Who cares if a couple of slimy barmen get their kicks out of tabulating their pathetic little love lives? Forget it, Anna. In two months' time, you'll be back in London and they'll be trying the same trick with two more innocent English girls. Getting a reputation in Crete hardly counts. Besides, you know you didn't do anything.'

'Yeah, but who's going to believe that?'

'So, we'll get disapproving looks from a few of the Greek grannies down in the village. Don't waste your time thinking about it. Unless, of course,' she added, cocking her head to one side inquisitively, 'you're actually worried about what Vangelis thinks of you.'

Anna took her coffee cup over to the sink and dropped it into the washing-up water. From the kitchen window, she could see Vangelis trudging up the hill towards the site where Dr Sillery had already been working for an hour.

'Don't be silly. Why should I be worried about what Vangelis thinks?' she asked.

Miranda simply shrugged and finished her toast.

Chapter Seven

But that day at the dig was tense. Though shards of pottery and other small pieces were turning up regularly, Dr Sillery was impatient to make the big breakthrough he was hoping for, since a really important find might help him to buy some more time from the big hotel developers. As a result, he snapped at Anna for being clumsy when she stumbled into one of the tables upon which he had laid out his finds for cataloguing. Nothing was broken, fortunately, but he still didn't speak to Anna for almost an hour afterwards, and kept muttering to himself about 'people', meaning Anna and Miranda, of course, not really having their hearts in the work.

As it was, that day Anna's heart wasn't really in anything. All she wanted to do was stretch out like a cat in the sun and catch up on the sleep she had missed since leaving London. The urge to close her eyes was totally overpowering by lunchtime, and within two minutes of the half hour Dr Sillery had so generously allowed them to eat their dry sandwiches, Anna was asleep in the shade of a low stone wall.

But not for long. She was just drifting into a delicious daydream about the fields around her childhood home when she was rudely shaken awake. Anna rubbed her eyes and sighed when Miranda's grin finally came into focus.

'You were doing it again,' Miranda smiled.

'What?'

'Moaning in your sleep. If I didn't know better, I'd say you were sex-starved and gagging for it.'

'I was dreaming about the fields outside my home town actually.'

Miranda pulled a face. 'Boring.'

'Not as boring as this bloody dig,' said Anna, as she left the shade of the wall and headed for the most isolated spot in the site. She needed some time to herself. But Miranda was determined to follow.

'I know what you mean. He's been really getting on my tits today,' she muttered as she sat down beside Anna and scraped aimlessly at a patch of dirt.

'Who?'

'Sillery. The way he keeps shouting at me, it's no wonder I dropped that pot a minute ago.'

'You dropped a pot? Did it break?'

'Yes, it did. But it was clearly late-twentieth-century terracotta so I think I just about got away with it. Spoken to Vangelis yet?'

'Not really. He said thank you when I passed him a bucket.'

'I thought he might have joined us for lunch, but apparently he had to meet someone in the village. Didn't say who, so it's probably a girl.'

'He is allowed.'

'Yeah. It's one rule for them though, isn't it? We go out to get ourselves some action and we're whores. When men do it, they're studs.'

'He might have gone to meet his mother.'

'No. I heard him talking to the man who delivers the bread in the mornings. My Greek is pretty rusty but I think he was discussing someone's tits. Perhaps they were yours.'

Anna rolled her eyes. 'Perhaps they were his mother's,' she added wickedly.

'You kill me, you do. Coming out again tonight?' Miranda asked, just as Dr Sillery started walking towards them to check that the hilarity coming from their comer of the site wasn't interfering with the job in hand.

'I don't think so,' Anna replied.

'OK,' said Miranda. 'Whatever you want. We can have a girls' night in instead.'

Chapter Eight

'Miranda,' Anna asked later that night, 'what do you think it takes to make a relationship work in the long term?'

'If you have to ask me that, then your relationship quite obviously isn't working,' said Miranda flatly.

'What do you mean?'

'I mean, you'll just know when you find the right one. You won't need to "work" at it at all. Until then, you shouldn't take things so seriously, Anna. You should have some fun.' Miranda got another beer out of the bucket of cold water she had placed next to the bed as a makeshift fridge. As promised, they were having a girls' night in, though Anna would really rather have been alone.

'Want another one of these?' Miranda asked.

'I don't think so. I think I've had enough.'

Miranda snorted. 'Enough? You've had two and you haven't even finished the second one. You haven't had enough at all. That's your problem, Anna. You never have enough. You're a control freak.'

'I don't think I am,' Anna squeaked.

'Control freaks never do. Here. Have another one.' Miranda pressed the bottle into Anna's hand, then lay back on the pillows and started to sip hers. Anna sipped at hers rather more slowly, still sitting stiffly on the edge of the bed, as though she wanted to be ready to flee.

'Are you comfortable like that?' Miranda asked after a while.

'Yes. I'm fine.'

'No, you're not. Come up here and sit against the pillows for heaven's sake.' Anna shuffled backwards. 'Isn't that better?' Anna nodded. For a while, they drank in silence. Then Miranda piped up again. 'Any progress with Vangelis?'

'No, of course there isn't,' Anna snorted. 'I mean, I haven't even been trying with him. I've got someone at home, remember.'

'Well, you know what I think about that. That relationship's over, Anna. If he didn't think he could keep himself on the straight and narrow while you spent just two little months over here, then he doesn't really care.'

'You don't pull any punches, do you?' Anna commented.

'I just don't like to see another girl wasting her time on someone who won't even waste the time it takes to text her.'

'Thanks a lot. Maybe he has texted but it can't get through here.'

'You're mum's texts are still getting through. I mean it, Anna.' Miranda turned towards her and laid a hand on her arm to take the sting out of her words. 'I mean, what's so special about this Justin guy that makes him think it's all right to treat you this way? You've sent him the landline number here. How dare he not phone up to see how you're getting on? Or even send you a poxy little email to say that he's sorry about the row but he misses you and can't wait until you come back? You're funny. You're gorgeous. You've got a great set of boobs.'

Anna tried to laugh but it came out as more of an anguished snort than a giggle. 'Oh, hey.' Miranda ran a hand across her new friend's cheek. 'You're not going to start crying on me, are you?' Anna shook her head but turned her face away from the caress all the same. 'I didn't mean to go over the top.'

'You didn't,' Anna promised, sniffing hard as she tried to compose herself. 'In fact, from what you know about Justin, everything you're saying makes perfect sense. But you know what it's like. I've seen great times with him as well as all the shit I've been getting recently. It's difficult to let all that good stuff go too.'

'Come here.' Miranda held out her arms and enfolded Anna against her bosom. 'What you need right now is a bit of human contact. It's enough to make anyone cry, two months with nothing to fondle but those rotten old Minoan pots.'

Anna laughed again, and this time it came out properly.

'What about you, Miranda?' she asked quickly to change the subject, subtly extracting herself from Miranda's grasp at the same time. 'Been thinking about the one you left behind?'

'Mmmm. On and off. Meeting that Nicky bloke the other night took my mind off him to a certain extent. Nicky's certainly miles better than my ex, Adam, in the body department. You know, sometimes I used to be having really great, wild sex with Adam, then I'd catch sight of a hair coming out of his ear or a whole bunch of them poking out of his nose and from then on he might as well have been poking me up the vagina with a cotton bud for all the arousal I felt . . . when he could get it up in the first place.'

Anna couldn't help laughing.

'It's not funny.'

'You made it sound that way. I've never been with an older man,' Anna admitted.

'Oh well.' Miranda smiled. 'You haven't missed much. It's like lamb and mutton. You know what's really best but when you're out in the sticks you have to put up with what's available.'

'But you weren't out in the sticks when you met your older man . . .'

'No. I suppose I wasn't. And without wishing to sound boastful, I'm pretty certain I could have had the pick of the undergraduates that year. But if I'm honest, Adam had something that made up for his tired old body. He is incredibly charming. Witty. Sophisticated. Tells a good dirty joke. I think he could have had any woman in that archaeology department and half the men as well.' Miranda's eyes focused into the distance as though she were seeing into the past.

'Sounds as though this man has affected you more than you want to admit,' Anna observed.

Miranda shrugged. 'Well, I didn't think it would

all end quite so suddenly. Seems like someone threatened to tip his wife off if he didn't stop seeing me pronto.'

'That's nasty. Any idea who?'

'Someone not a million miles from here.'

'Not Sillery?' Anna guessed.

'Perhaps.'

'I can't imagine he'd get involved with anything emotional.'

'Well, if he did, he'll be sorry.'

Anna almost shivered at the threat.

'He's not quite like I expected,' Anna continued. 'I thought he was supposed to be fat.'

'He was, until this year. Shame his character hasn't improved to match his body.'

'Do you think he's been working out since you last saw him?'

'No. I think it's just the excitement of this dig. Minoan relics give him a stiffy. He hardly eats anything these days either.'

'Not like Vangelis,' Anna observed.

'I know. Where does he put it all, eh? Though I

had a pretty good guess that first night. Felt like he was hung like that donkey we saw down in the village.' She laughed raucously.

Anna jumped up from the bed and went to the window to close it.

'Miranda! He might hear you.'

'He'd never guess we were talking about him. Vangelis is another one of those asexual artefact fiends. Very much mind over matter. I thought I was getting somewhere with him when he asked me into his room that first night, but all he wanted to do was show me his nicely bound thesis on Knossos. I had to promise that I'd read it before the end of this dig and he still wouldn't give me what I really wanted in return.'

Anna couldn't help smiling. 'He must be gay if he could resist you,' she joked.

'Mmmm,' said Miranda. 'Might be different for you, though. I've been thinking about that silly row you had with him, about the "love-boat". Something tells me that he was taking more than a brotherly interest in your welfare. In fact, I think he was rather jealous of poor old fishy Phil.' Miranda did a quick impression of ol' Cross-eyes.

'No,' said Anna, giggling at Miranda's face. 'I don't think so . . .'

'You walk around with your eyes shut,' sighed Miranda. 'It's perfectly obvious he fancies you. Small brunettes must be his type. Listen, if you're not going to drink up and tell me all your secrets, I might just have to sign up for another tour of duty on the *Ship of Whores*. Are you coming too?'

Anna shook her head.

'No, of course you're not. I'll see you in the morning.'

With that, she planted a kiss on the crown of Anna's head and left. Anna watched her from the window as she picked her way down the scrubby path to the village. When Miranda was out of sight, another silhouette appeared. The orange glow of a cigarette tip rose to the silhouette's mouth, then he seemed to turn from his view of the inky black sea to regard the house. It was Vangelis. Anna let the curtain fall shut again.

She sat down on the edge of the bed but she didn't get back under the covers. Whether Vangelis had been jealous of Phil or not, the tension between them since the breakfast debacle had been pretty uncomfortable. Perhaps she should go downstairs and talk to him right now. Nothing heavy. She didn't even need to mention the row. She'd just pretend that she needed a breath of fresh air and engage him in conversation about the dig as if that morning's uncomfortable exchange had never happened.

Anna slipped on her sandals and headed for the door, but, catching sight of herself in the mirror, she hesitated. She peered at her smooth round face in the reflection. Checked her teeth. Admired the slight suntan she had already picked up on her cheeks. Did it really bring out the green flecks in her hazel eyes? Then she caught herself worrying about what Vangelis would think of the way she looked, and reprimanded herself for her concern.

'He's just a colleague,' she murmured. 'It doesn't matter if your hair looks a mess.'

But by the time she got outside, Vangelis was nowhere to be seen anyway. Anna stood for a moment at the end of the garden path, scanning the scrub beyond the wall for the glow of his cigarette. Too late. Perhaps he had gone down to the taverna. Yes. He had gone to the taverna in pursuit of Miranda. How stupid Anna had been. It was Miranda he was really worried about, not Anna at all.

Anna returned reluctantly to her bedroom and slipped off her shoes again, feeling slightly daft and slightly embarrassed, though no one would ever know.

Up above her head, the fan turned lazily, stirring up a breeze, but it was still too hot to sleep. Anna's thin sundress was clinging to her curves with sweat. Unbuttoning the small mother-of-pearl buttons that stretched from neck to hem, she shrugged the dress off so that the fan could dry the moisture on her skin.

'Oh, Justin,' she sighed. 'Another seven and a half weeks of this agony before I can see you again. What am I supposed to do with myself until then?'

Anna rested her hand lightly over the silky triangle of her pubic hair. Perhaps she would have to get used to looking after herself. She almost smiled at the thought.

Slowly, she moved her long fingers down so that they were resting right on her clitoris. She was surprised to discover that she was already slightly damp between her legs. The heat, no doubt. Or was it the anticipation she had felt as she walked down into the garden in search of Vangelis?

Vangelis . . . Anna could picture him now as he had appeared to her on that first morning at the villa. She could imagine him smiling broadly as he poured coffee for breakfast. His chocolatey brown eyes, so attractively kind, echoed the happy curve of his mouth. She had never kissed a man with brown eyes, she suddenly smiled to herself. All her boyfriends had been geeky mousy mongrels, with light brown hair and grey eyes behind glasses – until Justin. In fact, there had been nothing particularly physically attractive about them at all. Anna's best school friend had always complained that Anna liked intellectuals, that she would never drop her principles and have a wanton week with someone that she fancied like mad, though they would have nothing to talk about afterwards.

Not that it would necessarily be like that with Vangelis. He wasn't some rugby-playing meat-head. But there was something disturbingly basic about him. Something ancient. Something animal. He exuded the kind of raw sexuality that Anna had always shied away from before.

Now she was thinking of him as he had been that morning. The smile gone. In its place, a certain hardness. Strangely, Anna found herself replaying that morning's uncomfortable scenario over and over again as she gently stroked her clitoris into arousal. Except that, in her imagination, once the argument was over Vangelis didn't walk away. Instead, he grabbed Anna's arm as she walked to the door, snapped her to him and pressed his lips against hers so hard it felt as though he might have bruised them.

His hand crunched up the back of her T-shirt as

he pulled her tight against him. His other hand ripped viciously at the button to her shorts. Before she knew what he was doing, his hand was inside her thin cotton panties, seeking out her clitoris. Then she felt a finger, pushing its way inside her. She felt powerless to do anything but give in to the cruel arousal; her vagina was wet in spite of him. She pressed her pubic bone hard against his hand and didn't complain as he edged her panties down.

His solid penis was already clearly outlined in the soft denim of his jeans. Anna held her hand against it, not knowing whether she should set it free. Vangelis had her panties around her knees now. He spun her around so that she fell roughly against the table, stretching her arms out just in time to save herself from going nose down in the butter. Behind her, she could hear the distinctive ripping sound of a zip being pulled down. Then Vangelis's hands were on her buttocks, pulling them roughly apart as he stepped forward and suddenly jammed his hot, hard shaft into her from behind.

Anna squealed with surprise as he rammed the first thrust home. Her legs trembled as he hammered his body against hers, so hard that it seemed to force the breath from her lungs. A super-powerful thrust sent her flying forward on to the tablecloth, knocking plates and cups and cutlery to the floor, a jangling accompaniment to Vangelis's moans and grunts.

Soon Anna knew that she was about to come in spite of herself. Her body seemed to be gathering itself with just one aim in mind. Vangelis held her firmly by the waist now, yanking her backwards to meet him as he powered forward. Her buttocks were damp with his sweat and her cum.

Just as he came, the kitchen door swung open. Miranda stood in the doorway, her eyes wide as the plates that lay smashed on the floor. Vangelis yanked Anna's head up by the hair so that she could see they had a visitor, just as she gave in to the first flood of her lust . . .

Back in the bedroom, Anna collapsed breathless on her pillows. She put her busy fingers, wet with her own juices, up to her lips. She licked them lasciviously, as though Miranda were really watching, as though Vangelis were still pulling himself slowly out of her. Anna gave one last delicious guilty shudder as the fantasy faded and she drifted into sleep.

Chapter Nine

Meanwhile, down in the taverna, Nicky the barman had been waiting impatiently for Miranda to arrive all evening. Phil had already given up on finding any action that night and gone home to bed. There had been no foreign girls at all in the taverna all night, and even if Miranda did turn up, Phil didn't hold out much hope for a night of passion with her frigid friend.

When Miranda parted the vines that overhung the taverna door and stepped inside, Nicky's eyes lit up like the stars they had watched from the boat the night before.

'I thought you weren't going to come to me,' he began. 'I have been waiting to see you all night.'

'I'll bet you have. I had a few things to sort out back at the villa,' Miranda explained. 'But I'm here now. Are we alone, my dear?'

'I closed the taverna early,' said Nicky, nodding quickly. 'Especially for you.'

'My my, we are keen,' Miranda purred as she slipped on to his warm lap and planted a kiss on his stubbly cheek.

'Miranda,' he murmured, returning her kiss with a greedy assault on her mouth while simultaneously sliding a hand beneath her skirt.

'Watch my lipstick,' she warned him, before standing up again to shrug off the cropped denim jacket she had worn to fend off the other biting creatures of the night.

Nicky licked his lips as Miranda sat back down astride him. She enveloped him in her perfumed arms and began to nibble gently at his ear. Nicky tipped his head back and Miranda planted a kiss on his Adam's apple. Nicky planted his hot hands on

Miranda's knees, and started to slide them up towards her thighs.

'Not here,' she told him, playfully pushing him away again. 'How about in the kitchen?'

'In the kitchen?' Nicky was surprised. 'You want to go in the kitchen?'

'Yes, I've always wanted to make love in a real professional kitchen. All that shining stainless steel. Nice and chilly. Really turns me on. Don't you feel the same way?'

Nicky shrugged. It was clear he'd never really thought about it.

'You could cover me with olive oil,' Miranda continued dreamily. 'It wouldn't be as much fun to lick off as melted chocolate, but I think we could have a very good time just sliding around on all those lovely shiny work surfaces. Come on, lover-boy. Take me next door. I'm absolutely ravenous for your body.'

Nicky looked hesitant.

'What's the matter, Nicky?' Miranda asked. 'Got something in there you don't want me to see?'

'No. I . . . er, I . . .'

'Then let's go, before I change my mind.' Miranda got to her feet and led Nicky by the collar to the gleaming kitchen. She left the door she pushed open propped wide so that she couldn't see the back of it. Nicky gulped as Miranda surveyed the little room, her eyes sweeping across the jars of ingredients towards the door. Surely she must shut it now and see what was behind.

'It's lovely in here,' she said. 'Just as I imagined it. Is it OK if I sit down on this?'

Miranda perched herself on the edge of the huge stainless steel work-table that dominated the centre of the room. Slowly, she lay back upon it until she was completely prone. A sly smile spread across her red lips. 'It's very cold,' she remarked, stroking the steel surface with her hands. 'But I like that. Makes me feel all tingly. Are you going to join me?' she asked Nicky. 'Why don't you come over here and close the door behind you?'

Nicky went to the door and fiddled around with the secret something that was obviously hanging from the back of it.

'What are you doing?' Miranda asked him with faux impatience.

'Er . . . nothing.' Nicky continued to fumble.

Miranda slid herself back into a sitting position and looked at Nicky with one eyebrow raised. 'Nothing? Then why are you so jumpy tonight? Are you hiding something from me? I think you are. Let me look.'

Before he could protest, Miranda had pushed Nicky aside and got her first look at what he was trying to hide behind the door. She couldn't help but laugh out loud when she discovered Vangelis had been right. Pinned straight into the wood of the door was a large paper chart ruled into two long columns. At the head of one column was Phil's name in red. At the head of the other was Nicky's.

'What is this?' Miranda asked rhetorically, as she began to scan down the list of names, looking frantically for hers, which she hoped would be the last one. There were literally hundreds of girls up there, but so many of them had no scores or very low ones, that Miranda felt confident in the knowledge that not all had succumbed. Finally she found her own name, alongside Anna's, which was the last name on Phil's side. Anna had a measly two, Miranda, an eight and a half.

'Nicky, I think you need to explain yourself,' Miranda told him sternly. 'Because I don't like the look of this. Not one little bit. Am I right to think that this is a list of all the girls you have slept with?'

Nicky had already coloured bright red.

'Because, you know,' Miranda continued, 'I don't like to think of myself as one of a crowd.'

'Er, that is not the case,' Nicky flustered. 'You could never be just one of many, my dear Miranda. You were special to me. You see,' he added, jabbing at her name. 'You are the last name on my list. There will never be another after you.'

'You don't have to pretend to me that that is even half true. But what really bothers me,' Miranda mused, with her finger on her score, 'is that there's a girl three lays before me who got herself a perfect ten. What did she do? Give you a blowjob while playing the *1812 Overture* with her fanny?'

'Eh?'

'Oh, forget it, Nicky. You've had your chance. I'm not hanging around to find out what it takes to get full marks from you, you jerk.'

Miranda made like she was just about to leave. She shrugged on her jacket and put her hand firmly on the door handle.

'It's a pity, Nicky. I could have forgiven you. But when I saw that measly eight and a half you'd given me up there? Well, that's just unforgivable in any girl's books.'

She began to stride out through the darkened taverna, heading for the door. 'I guess your *Ship of Whores* has just been sunk.'

'Wait, wait,' Nicky pleaded, chasing her out into the night-fragrant garden. 'Wait. I am sorry, Miranda. I am really sorry. I will never give a girl a mark for sex again. I swear to you. You will be the only one.'

'I wish I could believe that.'

'I want to make it up to you.'

'I don't know if you can.'

'I will. I promise.'

'How?' Miranda asked, narrowing her eyes.

'I'll do anything you like.'

'Anything?' Miranda paused by the wooden gate with a small smile playing on her lips. 'You know, Nicky, "anything's" a very dangerous ransom to promise a woman with a grudge.'

'I don't care. Just don't leave me here alone now. Miranda, please. I beg you. Stay. I need you. I think I love you.'

That really made her laugh. But suddenly Miranda turned and walked back into the taverna, straight through the bar and back into the kitchen, where she sat down once more on the edge of the stainless steel table. A little bit of a wriggle and she had slipped off her purple knickers from beneath her dress. She opened her legs elegantly to reveal a fluffy blond triangle of pubic hair, while the lacy panties floated to the floor like a dying butterfly.

'You know,' she sighed, 'it usually takes me so long to come by cunnilingus that I sometimes feel guilty even suggesting to a man that he brings me off that way. But I figure you really owe me one, Nicky. On your knees, boy.'

Nicky had no choice but to obey. With an uncertain look on his face, he knelt on the floor before Miranda and slid his hands up her legs to her thighs.

'You know what to do, I hope?' she asked.

Nicky nodded. He licked his lips, moistening them before moving in on her. Miranda was pleasantly surprised to find herself so full of anticipation. Her chest heaved as she began to breathe more heavily. Then she lay fully back on the table and made up her mind to simply relax and enjoy and not feel at all guilty, however long it took the poor boy to finish the job . . .

Like a snake searching for its prey, Nicky darted his tongue out of his mouth to make the first tender contact with Miranda's beautiful cunt. He was so delicate at first that she could hardly feel him, but when she did, the thrill that went through her body was electric.

'Harder, Nicky,' she murmured, placing her hand on the back of his head and pushing him further down.

Soon Nicky was getting into his stride. This time, the pressure of his tongue was so much stronger that

Miranda didn't last two seconds before she felt the urge to squirm. But more was to come. He sucked at her clitoris, taking it right into his mouth as no one had ever done before. To Miranda, it felt as if her clit had suddenly sent out a network of nerve tentacles that covered her entire lower body, tracks of ecstasy that reached down the inside of her legs to be raced along by bolts of electricity that came each time Nicky's tongue hit the button. Miranda was soon crawling backwards up the table, her fingers grabbing vainly at the stainless steel as she writhed in the joyous agony of passion. As she tried to slip away from him, Nicky grasped her waist in his powerful hands to pull her back down towards his tongue.

'Oh no, oh no, oh no!' Miranda panted. She was shocked to discover that she felt as though she couldn't possibly wait any longer. But then Nicky's tongue was replaced by two fingers. He licked them first for extra lubrication.

Nicky began to slide his fingers rhythmically in and out of her soaking vagina. He worked slowly at first, then faster and faster and faster. Miranda thrashed her head from side to side on the stainless steel table, moving her hips down to meet his fingers at each thrust. Her breath escaped from her open mouth in short gasps, punctuated by cries for mercy – which she didn't really want. Opening her eyes briefly, she saw, and heard, that Nicky too was panting. His face was flushed, his pupils wide with pleasure, as he continued to work in and out of her vagina, pausing only to massage her engorged clitoris with his thumb.

'Oh no, oh no!' Miranda sat up suddenly. This really was too much. She clamped her hand like a vice around Nicky's wrist and held his fingers deep within her as the first waves of her orgasm began to build inside her. Stars danced behind her eyelids. The sound of the hot blood rushing around her head filled her ears like the roar of an angry sea.

'Aaaaah . . .' Her grip tightened as an orgasm exploded deep within her, flooding her limbs with pins and needles. Blood raced from one extreme of her body to another, leaving her shuddering and moaning and shaking in its wake, until finally her grip on Nicky's aching hand relaxed and her body slumped backwards on to the table. Finished. Wasted. Exhausted. But satisfied.

When she had gathered herself again, Miranda sat up and looked at her cruel Greek lover. Nicky was leaning against the door to the kitchen, right against his lover's league list, and looking very proud of himself as he lit up a cigarette.

'You cheated,' said Miranda as she straightened herself up. 'That wasn't full cunnilingus. But it wasn't bad either.' She had to admit that.

'Am I forgiven?' he asked her. 'Will you come back here again?'

Miranda picked her panties up from the filthy kitchen floor and wriggled them back on. She made for the door and gently pushed Nicky out of her way so that she could pass through it.

'Will you come back tomorrow?' he asked her once more. Desperately, she thought.

'If I can think of another use for you . . . perhaps,' she said.

Then she kissed him on the cheek and left.

Chapter Ten

Miranda sauntered back up the dark pathway to the villa. Anna was still awake, sitting by her bedroom window, looking out into the darkness for the fishing boat lights that added glitter to the sea, like a fisherman's wife waiting for her husband's return after a terrible storm.

Not noticing Miranda's return, Anna was surprised to hear the door creaking open. Miranda stood in the doorway, silhouetted by the light from the hall.

'Can't sleep again?' she asked.

Anna nodded.

'Mind if I join you over there?'

The two girls sat together at the window in the darkness, saying nothing.

Anna continued to watch the sea, but after a while she sensed that Miranda's eyes were not upon the view but upon her. Anna turned to catch Miranda studying her intensely. She was staring at Anna with a look of plain intent in her eyes that Anna had only ever previously seen in the eyes of a man.

Anna swallowed nervously as Miranda's liquid gaze continued to pierce her eyes. The muscles at the back of her neck twisted with the tension of this endless moment while each girl wondered what would happen next. Only Miranda had a much better idea of what was coming.

Moving imperceptibly closer, Miranda brushed her ruby lips across Anna's cheek. Anna's eyes widened with shock. The sensation of this unexpected action of affection was not of the lightest of kisses but of a burning firebrand. Miranda sat back

to look at Anna and a moment of silence and still-
ness hung between them once more before she
finally drew Anna's lips to her own.

Anna had never kissed another woman before
and when Miranda placed her slender, well-
manicured hand on Anna's knee, Anna's first
instinct was to pull away. But for Miranda this was
definitely not a first time. The surprise Anna thought
she had seen in her friend's eyes was merely pleasure at the arrival of such a delicious unexpected
opportunity. Miranda passed a casual hand over
Anna's dark hair, silvered with moonlight, as
though she were calming an anxious pet cat.

'Don't think about it too much,' Miranda whispered. 'Just let it happen. You'll like this. I promise
you.'

Anna closed her eyes tightly, shutting out the face
that drew closer to her own. Miranda persisted,
kissing Anna softly on her jaw, her chin, her nose,
her ears, her eyelids, her forehead and then on her
soft pink lips again. Finding Anna's lips still tightly
shut after all this gentle persuasion, Miranda made

a little noise of amusement before she set to work at prising them open with her tongue. Moments later Anna's own tongue poked out tentatively to touch the tip of Miranda's. This kiss was different from any kiss Anna had experienced before. Miranda's touch was lighter and gentler than any man's. Her breath was sweet, like flowers, her skin as smooth as satin.

Miranda drew away from Anna again to check her eyes for distress, laughing slightly to herself. Sure now that Anna wasn't about to scream and run away, Miranda led her from the window seat to the bed and gently pushed her backwards on to it. However, Anna's body was so stiff with tension that Miranda was reminded of a china doll she had had as a child. And as the kissing continued, Anna kept her eyes tightly shut, still wrestling with the fact that she was being seduced by a woman.

But soon a warm hand was creeping beneath Anna's soft white T-shirt, caressing through her old cotton bra a nipple that was hardening in spite of Anna's misgivings. Anna let Miranda's hands wander curiously over her body for a moment or two, unsure of what she should be doing in return. She had guessed that she should probably be doing exactly the same as Miranda was doing to her, but the move from kissing another woman to actually caressing her eager, feminine body seemed just too great a move to make right then. So Miranda had to be patient for a while, content just to be nuzzling Anna's suntanned cheeks, whispering sweet little words of pleasure and encouragement until she felt Anna's arms finally close around her back and knew that she had broken through.

Miranda was far from shy herself. She had struggled out of her skimpy top at the earliest possible opportunity and happily lay her half-naked torso against Anna's. She had already pushed Anna's clothing out of the way so that their bodies rested in some places skin to skin, though Anna felt that her nakedness was more than just skin-deep.

'Touch me, Anna,' Miranda murmured hotly, 'touch me too.' Her commanding words were softened by her quickening breath. Anna moved a tentative hand from Miranda's back in the direction of her ample breasts. Miranda shifted eagerly to make herself perfectly accessible. She held herself slightly above Anna and to her side, jutting out her perfect breasts like fleshy battlements so that the target for attention couldn't be more obvious.

Miranda's breasts were prettily encased in a peach-coloured lace-edged bra that was almost invisible against her lightly sunkissed skin. Anna began to caress them, in the way that Miranda had caressed hers, but it soon became clear that Miranda was happy to take things more quickly because, before Anna could gather up the courage to tuck her hand inside the bra and actually touch Miranda's delicate nipples, the blonde girl had reached around and unhooked her own bra herself.

'Kiss them,' Miranda begged her nervous new lover, 'suck them. You can even lick them if you like. They're yours.' Tentatively, Anna lifted her head to the proffered breast and flicked out her warm, wet tongue. Miranda's tiny pink nipples had stiffened immediately at the mere suggestion of Anna's caress.

She pulled Anna's head closer to her breast and thrust one of the quivering buds into Anna's mouth. 'Bite it,' she commanded softly. Part of Anna's mind still fought against the suggestion but she soon found that she had gently closed her teeth together on the stiff little bud. 'Harder,' Miranda rasped, as she felt the delicious pain send bolts of arousal through her body. 'Bite them a little bit harder.'

As Anna paid attention to her lover's breasts, Miranda's hands had crept lower. She was wrestling with the belt of Anna's tatty shorts, deftly unfastening the button fly and tugging the denim down. Suddenly noticing the shift in focus, Anna felt herself flick back to full consciousness and tried to push the fiddling hands away.

'No, don't,' she pleaded. 'I really don't think I want . . .'

'This?' It was too late. Miranda ran her hands over Anna's naked torso, and the hair on the back of Anna's neck seemed to stir with excitement as Miranda's fingers brought her up in goosebumps of nervous desire.

Anna closed her eyes as Miranda's fingers tangled in her pubic hair, waiting for the inevitable. Soft but insistent fingers on her clitoris made her bite her lip as the sensation sent tiny arrows of tingling electricity all over her body. Miranda kissed Anna again, thrusting her tongue inside Anna's sweet, warm mouth as her fingers echoed the action down below.

'Wait!' Anna broke away from her lover's mouth and threw back her head. This was too much. Just too much.

'Sssssssh,' Miranda whispered. 'Don't panic, my darling. You're so nice and warm inside. So wet, so ready. You're enjoying this. You really are.' A peculiar tingle ran down Anna's spine at these words. 'Just lie back and relax and wait. I'm going to make you come all over me . . . You don't have to do a thing.'

The words, so quiet yet so commanding, stripped Anna of the last of her inhibitions. Automatically now, Anna raised her hips so that Miranda could pull her shorts completely out of the way. Beneath them, Anna was wearing just a flimsy white thong, as she often did in the heat. Miranda smiled her approval as she pulled the tiny bit of cotton out of the way, licked her lips wickedly as she contemplated the task ahead, and ducked her glossy head down between Anna's thighs.

With the first expert flick of her tongue, Miranda found Anna's long-dormant clitoris. Anna bucked her hips upwards with the surprise of the perfect hit and while they were thus raised, Miranda grabbed her lover's buttocks and used them to lift the girl still further, so that she could more easily reach her target. Her tongue moved fairly slowly at first, up and down the shiny shell-pink skin of Anna's vulva, tantalising her clitoris. Miranda's eyes were fixed on Anna's all the time. Every cell in Anna's body was beginning to go into meltdown. Her nerves were frying with sensation.

'Let go of your fear,' Miranda demanded. 'Let yourself come with me. I can feel you're almost there.'

Miranda's face was wet from her nose to her chin and Anna knew that it wasn't all saliva. When

Miranda returned to her frantic tonguing this time, Anna's hips bucked ever higher again, as if to drive Miranda's tongue into her. Anna grasped the blonde head of her lover, forcing Miranda's face further down between her shaking thighs and at last Miranda knew that she wasn't going to have to ask Anna to come again.

Suddenly, Anna's body took over. Every muscle inside her was tensing and relaxing, tensing and relaxing so quickly it was as if she had been plugged into some ecstatic source of electricity. Resistance was no longer an issue as Anna's mind sat back, as if to watch her body as she shuddered and groaned and covered Miranda's face with sticky, sweet cum.

Anna's first Sapphic orgasm was over. When she had finished shaking with its tremendous power, Miranda crawled up the bed to lie beside her and kissed her gently on the mouth. Slowly Anna licked her swollen lips dry, tasting her own love-juice mingled with the taste of cigarettes and alcohol on Miranda's sweet wet tongue.

Later, when Miranda lay still on the shambles of a bed, her eyes closed in a contented doze, Anna wandered over to the bare dressing table and sat down. Her mouth and chin were smeared all over with Miranda's vibrant pink lipstick.

As she wiped her face clean again, Anna studied the reflection of the body lying behind her on the bed for a moment. Miranda's arms were raised above her head. Her body made a smooth unbroken curve that ran from the tips of her slender fingers to the soles of her feet, gently undulating in a perfect wave where a tiny waist became a swelling hip. Anna walked over to the bed and sat down beside her. Miranda's eyelids fluttered delicately as the bed dipped slightly beneath Anna's weight. Anna let the back of her fingers follow the line she had made with her eyes.

The gentle touch awoke Miranda, smiling, from her sleep, and she wrapped her arms around Anna's waist, pulling her down to lie beside her on the bed. They just looked at each other for a long time, noses almost touching as they lay face to face on the pillows, gently caressing each other's hair, ear lobes and cheeks, still flushed pink with arousal. Anna couldn't help but marvel at the fragility of the feminine body that had just given her such strong pleasure, stronger pleasure than she had ever received from a man, while outside the thick stone walls of the villa, the sea still caressed the stones on the shore as if nothing had changed.

'Are you OK?' Miranda asked. The expression on Anna's face was still that of someone who was not sure that she had done the right thing. Anna didn't know how to answer and so she simply grinned.

'Are you OK?' Miranda asked again. 'It's eight a.m., Anna. Old Sillery is already on the war path. I really can't afford to be late again this morning and neither, I think, can you. Get up, Sleeping Beauty. Rise and shine. Let's seize the day.'

Anna sat up in bed, rubbing the sight back into her sleep-blind eyes. What was Miranda doing by the door in her filthy overalls and working boots? Only seconds before she had been lying naked in the bed.

Except that Miranda hadn't ever been in Anna's bed, of course.

'My God,' sighed Anna as she forced herself not to slide back under the covers for another forty winks. 'I was having a seriously weird dream.'

'Really?' Miranda smiled. 'Well, you'll have to tell me about it later. I could do with a laugh. Right now though, I'm going to fix myself some breakfast. Staying up all night with Nicky has made me ravenous.'

'You were with Nicky?'

'Yeah. Of course. I told you where I was going.'

'Yeah. You did.' Anna watched Miranda go before slumping back on to her pillows. The eroticism of her dream was fading fast in the morning light but surreptitiously, Anna slipped a hand down between her thighs and found to her guilty surprise that she was still wet inside.

Did this mean she had feelings for Miranda?

Surely not. And even if she did, Anna told herself, it wasn't as if they would ever be reciprocated. Miranda Sharpe was the biggest man-eater since *Jaws*. With the emphasis on *man*.

Anna dragged her unwilling body from the bed and pulled on the pair of denim shorts that Miranda had so casually relieved her of in the dream. She shook her head at her reflection in the mirror. All this pent-up sexual frustration leaking out night after night. It couldn't be good for her, keeping it all inside. That evening, she decided, when work was over, she would write to Justin. No text or email but a properly handwritten letter that would remind him of what they were both missing and definitely persuade him to write back. If not actually visit.

At breakfast, Miranda asked Anna about her dream.

'Oh, it was nothing. I can hardly remember it now,' Anna lied.

'Bet it was a really dirty one in that case,' Miranda laughed in reply.

Chapter Eleven

'Dear Justin . . .'

Anna hid herself away after dinner that night to write the letter that would get her relationship with Justin back on the right track again. She chewed her pen as she wondered exactly how she should begin. She'd already decided that she had to make it sexy but should she look to the past and describe the best sex they had had so far in their relationship, or should she look to the future and describe the kind of mind-blowing sex they could have if only he would fly out to meet her in Crete?

She plumped for the latter. She decided that she would write a letter that would have him booking a ticket to Crete as soon as he had finished reading the first paragraph.

'Dear Justin,' she began. 'It's been almost two weeks since I left London for Crete. Two weeks too long without you here beside me. As I write this letter in my stark lonely room overlooking the ever-restless ocean, I can't help but wonder how different things would be if you were here with me now. This bed, which feels too wide for me alone, seems to ache almost as much as I do to have you lying here beside me tonight.

'Closing my eyes, I imagine you walking up the path to the villa and surprising me as I drift in and out of a restless sleep. To see you here would be so much like a dream that I would have to rub my eyes to convince myself that you were really here standing in front of me. And when I discovered that I wasn't dreaming, I would get such a rush of joy that it would leave me dizzy and unable to speak.

'But there would be no need for words to tell you how much I have missed you, dear Justin. Instead, I would throw myself straight into your arms and cover your beloved face with kisses. You in turn would hug me close to you, finally defeating the distance that has come between us, and poke your tongue into my mouth, a prelude to what would happen next.

'Still kissing you like a woman lost in the desert greeting water, I would lead you to my bedroom. The sheets on the bed, which now feel so cold against my lonely skin, would suddenly seem inviting. You would sit down upon the bed first and I would sit upon your knees, running my fingers through your beautiful golden hair as you kissed me till my lips felt as though they were bleeding with desire.

'Show me how much you have missed me, I would beg you. And you would race to show me right away. As I write, I can almost feel your strong warm hands slipping beneath the hem of my flimsy little sundress to caress my longing thighs. I, in turn, would be eager to see your beautiful body again. Tantalisingly slowly for both of us, I would begin to unbutton your faded shirt, revealing inch by inch your strong, broad chest and the soft curly hair that I love so much curving down towards your belly button like a path to lead me to your erection.

'Yes, you would have an erection already. And you would press my hand to it, drawing my attention there, as if I couldn't see it straining at the front of your trousers. I would pull down the zipper, extra slowly just to punish you, and set your aching penis free. While you lay back on the pillows, I would turn my attention to your feet, untying and discarding your shoes, then kissing the arch of your beautiful soles, before wriggling your trousers free from your hips and sliding them off you and on to the floor.

'When you were finally completely naked, I would crawl on to the bed again and drag myself up the mattress towards you. Imagine my breasts, Justin, swollen with desire for you, falling forward as I bend over your body to take your throbbing shaft between my lips. Closing my eyes to think of you now, I can almost feel you touching my nipples, gently twisting them into hardness as I suck at your long, hard penis. Down below, my labia would start to swell and pulsate with anticipation. I want you so much. I can hardly wait. But we would have to make the moment last, make it truly special.

'Next, your eager fingers would wander over my naked buttocks to seek out the opening to my most secret place. The fact that I am already wet when you get there makes you smile. But I am always wet for you. You know how to make me drip with desire without even touching me at all. Just the thought . . . just the thought of you beside me is enough. I'm wet right now just thinking about it, even though you're miles away from me.

'But your strong clever fingers would quickly bring me to the edge. You always stroke my clitoris so confidently. You know what to do. You always know what to do. Then you would thrust a finger deep inside me. Can you imagine my vagina contracting around you as if in welcome? I long to pull you deep inside.

'But you would take your finger out of me and watch my face flush red as you licked your finger clean dramatically. You love the taste of me. And I love the taste of you, as I lick a bead of clear salty semen from the tip of your rock-solid shaft.

'Slowly, I would stroke you ever harder. My tongue would tease the eye of your shaft, while my fingers played teasingly with the soft orbs of your balls. I can see your proud penis twitching upwards towards me, like a racehorse waiting for the moment when the race is finally started. You would murmur how much you want me. I want you too, Justin. More than words can ever show.

'And when I could not possibly wait any longer to have you, I would push you back on to the pillows, then climb astride you. I would savour the smile on your handsome face as I hovered just a fraction of an inch above your penis, teasing you with the thought of what comes next.

'I can almost feel you sliding slowly inside me. I shudder with joy at the thought of you filling me up, touching me deep inside where no other man has ever touched me. I belong to you totally, Justin. Every part of my aching body is yours.

'Imagine us moving. Imagine the way I would ooze up and down you in measured strokes aimed to tease you to new heights of desire. Imagine my tanned thighs taut with the effort of moving my body so slowly. Imagine the agony of the orgasm building like a thunderstorm inside you. Imagine the climax we would have together after being so long without each other. There is an orgasm deep inside me which has been gathering strength and momentum for two whole weeks.

'Only you can set it free, Justin. I miss you. I love you. Crete just isn't hot enough without you. Please come to me soon.'

Anna smiled as she signed her name at the bottom of this letter of love, then she slipped it inside an envelope drenched with her perfume and, as the final touch, sealed the envelope with a pink lipstick kiss. She wondered how long it would take to reach her lover. Five days. Maybe a week, if she was very unlucky. Then Justin would know how much she had missed him. She had already decided that once they were reunited, as they surely must be after this filthy missive, she would never let herself be parted from him again.

Chapter Twelve

With the letter safely hidden inside the top drawer of her dressing table, Anna returned to bed. The window was open, and a cool breeze lifted the curtains like a veil, but writing to Justin had heated Anna up all over, and it seemed like she would never cool back down.

She was still awake, and thinking of the sex she had written about when, at two in the morning, she heard the front door to the villa creak open. It would be Miranda, no doubt returning from a spin around the bay on the love-boat. All right for some, thought Anna. Miranda never went without. But then, she wasn't what you could call 'choosy'. Anna waited to hear Miranda's not-so-sensible shoes clip-clopping up the marble stairway, but instead, the footsteps hesitated at the bottom step, and soon Miranda was clip-clopping towards Anna's room.

Anna wondered whether she should pretend to be asleep when the door to her room creaked open. But over the past couple of weeks she had learned that resistance to Miranda's midnight visits was pretty much useless. If Miranda wanted to talk to you, she talked, no matter what time of day or night it was. Soon she had installed herself at the bottom of Anna's bed, flipped off her shoes, and was massaging her feet back to life.

'My feet are killing me,' she whined.

'Well, I don't know how you've managed to get away without a broken ankle so far,' Anna observed dryly.

'Me neither. Though a fat lot of good my slapper shoes did me tonight.'

'How was Nicky?'

'I don't bloody well know. He wasn't there. I spent the whole evening drinking that vile paint-stripper stuff with your friend fishy Phil. Apparently Nicky went into Heraklion to fetch some supplies for the taverna this afternoon. Phil kept saying that Nicky would be back soon, but I think he was just hoping that I would stick around and drink enough raki to get desperate enough for a roll in the hay with him instead.'

'And you didn't?' Anna smiled.

'Credit me with some taste, please. Even I have some standards. Besides, I don't want your sloppy seconds.'

'I never even touched him!' Anna protested.

'I believe you,' said Miranda, but she couldn't help laughing at the thought of such a nasty match as she flopped backwards on to the bed beside Anna. As she hit the mattress, they heard the sound of paper crumpling, and soon Miranda had managed to find a stray page from Anna's first draft of the letter to Justin. Before Anna could snatch it back, Miranda was reading out loud.

'"Imagine how wet I am getting,"' she purred coquettishly. '"I long to feel you deep inside." Anna Hazel, what is this smut?'

'I was writing to Justin,' Anna said defensively. 'And it's private. Give it back, please.'

'No way, this is great reading. "I can almost feel your hot breath on my neck as you kiss me into submission." Mmm, Anna, you sly old fox! Are you writing this from experience, you lucky thing? Is this what he's really like in the sack?'

'Sometimes. Look, just give it back now, please, Miranda.'

Anna made a grab for the sheet of paper again, but Miranda was quicker and flipped it out of the way so that Anna ended up face down on the bedspread. When she had righted herself, Anna went for the paper again, but this time Miranda whipped the sheet over her head, so that Anna ended up on her back.

'Give it to me!' Anna shrieked. Miranda rolled out of reach once more. But only once more. The next time Anna made a dive for her letter, Miranda stayed quite still, so that Anna, expecting further evasory tactics, instead ended up right on top of her. Nose to nose. Within kissing distance.

Anna sat back up quickly, blushing like a beet-root, and ripped the page she had managed to retrieve into shreds. Miranda propped herself up on the pillows and smiled a slow smile.

'I wish someone would write me a letter like that,' she commented.

'Yeah? Well, you have to deserve one.'

'Don't I look like I deserve one?' Miranda pouted.

'I'm not going to answer that.' Anna walked across the room to put the shreds of discarded paper into her wastebin. But when she walked back towards the bed, she had a sudden giddy sense of déjà vu. Miranda was looking at her with *that* expression. The filthy expression she had had on her face at the beginning of *that* crazy dream.

'What's the matter?' Miranda asked, seeing Anna's own expression change with the realisation. 'You look like you've seen a ghost.'

'I have, sort of. But it's more like déjà vu!

'Weird. Please explain.'

'No.'

'Oh, I hate it when people do that,' Miranda sighed. 'If you've got an interesting story, tell it. Don't just raise my hopes and then button your lip.'

Anna gave a snorty little laugh. 'Well, you know that dream I had last night . . .'

'The dirty one?' asked Miranda eagerly.

'I never said it was dirty!'

'You didn't have to. I could tell just by looking at the state of your bedclothes when I interrupted you.'

'Well, it's just that walking across the room just then, everything looked exactly as it did in my dream last night. Or rather, you did.'

'I was in your dream?' said Miranda, without bothering to disguise her pleasure at the thought. 'My God, what was I doing?'

Anna sat down at her dressing table and looked at her face in the mirror, all mysterious in the blue-black shadows.

'Anna, you weren't having a filthy dream about me, were you?' Miranda probed.

Anna shared a secret smile with her reflection, but quickly supressed the grin when she turned back to her friend.

'You were,' Miranda shrieked. 'I knew it!'

'You knew it?' Anna exclaimed, turning back to face the mirror and hide her blushes. 'How could you know? You're so presumptuous.'

'And accurate?' Miranda sprawled across the sheets in what was, to her mind, her most seductive pose.

'Yeah. But it was just a dream,' Anna tutted. 'You'd better go to bed.'

'Perhaps you'd better come to bed, lover-girl,' said Miranda mischievously, narrowing her eyes and regarding Anna coquettishly from beneath her long eyelashes.

Anna laughed nervously as Miranda pouted her sex-kitten pout.

'You've never been to bed with a woman in real life, have you?' Miranda asked perceptively.

'Is it that obvious?' said Anna sarcastically.

'Well, you don't know what you've been missing.'

'You mean you have?'

'Maybe. Once or twice. It's really no big deal,' she added flatly.

Then Miranda got up from the bed, picked up her silly shoes and made for the door. But before she left the room, she couldn't resist reaching out to stroke Anna's hair in passing. Shaking the gesture off, Anna stood up from the table to close the door behind her visitor, and Miranda seized her chance. Before Anna could protest, Miranda had silenced her by sticking her tongue in Anna's mouth.

When Miranda finally let her go again, Anna was too shocked to complain.

'Easy, isn't it?' Miranda smiled. 'And no stubble.'

Anna just stood there, her mouth slack with surprise.

'You look like you've swallowed a goldfish. Come here.' Miranda went to kiss her again. And this time she took it more slowly. She cupped the back of Anna's head with her free hand and made a careful exploration of Anna's full pink lips with her tongue. Soon Anna heard the sound of Miranda's stilettos dropping to the floor, and Miranda's other hand started to creep up her back beneath the scruffy grey T-shirt that Anna had been wearing for bed.

Suddenly the question of whether this Sapphic encounter was going to be a good thing or not became academic. Anna knew that she was in the arms of someone she felt strongly sexually attracted to, whatever her sex, and to relax and let the moment take over seemed natural, the right thing to do.

Hesitantly at first, Anna wrapped her arms around Miranda's back, echoing her lover's more experienced movements. When Miranda's hand moved to Anna's breast, Anna soon found herself doing the same to Miranda's.

Miranda kicked the door, which had been left slightly ajar, shutting it with her foot and carefully guiding Anna back to the bed. They sat down upon the mattress and lay back upon the pillows slowly, still kissing as they moved. Anna's head touched the pillow at the exact moment Miranda's fingers breached the elastic of her flimsy cotton knickers.

'Miranda,' Anna exclaimed suddenly. 'I don't think . . .' But Miranda just put her finger to Anna's lips in reply. Anna closed her eyes as Miranda began to inch Anna's knickers down over her hips. The heat of Miranda's breath on her neck made Anna think that it must be leaving burn marks. Where Miranda's fingers touched her naked flesh, Anna imagined her pale skin turning bright red on contact.

'Touch me back,' Miranda pleaded. Anna had been so wrapped up in the novelty of this illicit sensation that she had become frozen upon the mattress. Snapping back into reality, she stroked a hesitant hand across Miranda's shoulder and down over her back. While Anna had been lying still with her eyes tightly shut, Miranda had shrugged her way out of her dress and was now naked but for a silky red thong that might as well have been made of a postage stamp for all the flesh it covered. Everything was happening so quickly.

Miranda sighed with pleasure as Anna's fingers brushed lightly over her softly curved buttocks. Anna could see now why Miranda always had such good luck with men. Her body was perfect. Like a Vargas pin-up girl. Anna could imagine Miranda's image painted on to the nose of a World War Two fighter plane. So different from Anna's own body. With her slim hips and long thin legs, Anna could slide easily between masculine and feminine. Not Miranda though. She was all woman.

Without a word of warning, Miranda dipped her head to the naked triangle of Anna's pubis and began to nuzzle softly at the silky fur of her pubic hair. While Anna stroked Miranda's beautiful blonde mane, Miranda slipped her long delicate fingers between Anna's legs and started to echo the strokes on Anna's clitoris. The sensation was exquisite. Anna's only other real lover had been Justin, and this was so different from making love to him.

Justin was always forceful, dominant. Miranda, by contrast, was gentle but insistent, coercing and coaxing the right reaction from Anna's body rather than forcing it. Anna had grown so used to Justin's powerful thrusting that she had forgotten how nice it was to be touched as though her body was a piece of rare porcelain. She rather liked the idea of herself as a beautiful vase. Delicate. Valuable. Cherished.

But Miranda soon started to quicken the pace. Anna gasped as Miranda slipped two fingers into her vagina and began to move them back and forth, gathering speed with her thrusting until Anna's whole body started to hum.

Anna thrashed her head from side to side upon the pillow in protest. She scrunched up great handfuls of sheet and creased it in her fists. It was just like the dream, right down to the musky sweet scent of arousal that was beginning to swirl about the room, as the heat of their twisting bodies sent the natural perfume of their skin drifting into the air above them.

Miranda took her fingers from Anna's vagina and sat back on her heels, examining the devastation she had managed to wreak so quickly on Anna's pathetic defences. Anna lay wide-eyed, panting, longing for Miranda to carry on, but still not quite able to ask for exactly what she wanted. Fortunately, Miranda was pretty good at guessing.

With a wicked smile playing across her perfect pout, Miranda slid back down the bed so that her heart-shaped face was level with Anna's pubis once more. Then, she carefully parted Anna's legs so that the glistening entrance to her vagina lay exposed.

Miranda stuck out her tongue, luxuriously, lasciviously, and began to lick. She started her attack with slow, deliberate strokes along the full length of Anna's vulva. Tender-tough strokes carefully designed to drive a woman insane. Anna didn't know what to do with herself. Should she close her eyes? Or should she let herself be flooded through all her senses? Where should she put her hands? In the end, she opted for touching her own breasts, toying with her own hardened nipples while Miranda worked her into ecstasy below.

Anna knew already that this would be an orgasm to put all those she had had before in the shade. Her body was trembling like an autumn leaf waiting to fall. It was as if all the blood in her veins was being concentrated into the tiny space beneath her skin, making each time Miranda touched her so intense that it was almost painful. Anna's internal organs felt as though they were dissolving. She was sure that if her heart pounded any faster, it would explode through her chest like the sudden blooming of a dark red rose.

Miranda took no notice of Anna's pathetic requests that she stop. Anna felt herself losing control of her limbs. Her body was on full sexual alert, and all the emergency troops were at her vagina. She gripped the top of Miranda's shoulders, leaving white fingermarks that quickly turned red when she was forced to let go by the sensation that suddenly overtook her.

She felt like a tiny fish that had found itself caught up in the crest of a gigantic wave. It was pointless to try and swim against it. The only thing she could do now was let her body go limp while the wave reached its maximum velocity and hit the shore, crumbling. But even then there was no respite, for even as Anna drew a gasping breath, she was being pulled back under by the next wave. And the next one and the next one. And the next . . . It felt as if this tremendous orgasm would never be over. Little by little, the waves that racked her body began to decrease in size and she was left gasping for air on the sand, like a flounder. Miranda held herself high above Anna's body, her face glowing with triumph. She had taken Anna to the very point of ultimate vulnerability and dropped her right off the edge of the earth.

Anna knew what would come next. Just as at the end of the dream. It was her turn to make love to Miranda. And it was unlikely that Miranda would want to save the event for another day, though it was so late that the first pale glow of dawn was creeping over the horizon like a thief.

It was the first time that Anna had ever seen another woman's vagina except in photographs. Miranda had rolled off Anna and reclined on the bed beside her, nonchalantly, her tanned legs slightly parted, just waiting for Anna to come between them and return the favours owed. Miranda's pubic hair was slightly darker than the hair on her head – and the darker hairs were already slightly damp. Anna found herself strangely pleased to discover that she hadn't been the only one to enjoy her first taste of true Sapphic lust.

'What are you waiting for?' Miranda asked provocatively, eyebrows raised in that 'come hither' look that had melted men in just about every comer of the earth.

A picture of Justin lying on another bed in another country flashed briefly through Anna's mind. Anna knew that this was infidelity. She knew that she should tell this woman to leave her room right now, but even as she was thinking that, she found herself transfixed as Miranda slowly slid herself forward so that her feet touched the floor and her cunt was at the edge of the bed. Then she reached out her hand and twisted a little of Anna's long brown hair between her fingers to bring her to heel. Miranda's face was glowing with desire. Even without words she was communicating a message that Anna could not ignore.

Anna knelt on the floor at the foot of the bed, between Miranda's open knees, and stared in wonder for a moment at the gently swelling clitoris and labia, which were becoming more prominent through the silky hair even as she drew nearer.

'That's right,' Miranda breathed. She pulled gently on Anna's hair to bring her closer still.

Anna gazed at the picture of feminine beauty before her. What should she touch her new lover with first? Her fingers or her tongue? Anna thought of the calluses on her hands caused by a hard day's digging and chose her tongue for its softness.

She began by carefully taking some of Miranda's soft, dark blonde curls between her teeth, nibbling and pulling at them gently, but not too hard. Miranda moaned contentedly and raised her hips slightly from the bed, letting Anna know that she was doing OK. The potent female aroma that Anna had often smelled on her own fingers after masturbating was rising gently towards her from Miranda's vagina, enticing Anna further down. Taking Miranda's curvaceous hips in her shaking hands,

Anna made her first move, stretching out her pink tongue to its full, hard length, licking and then penetrating. Tasting that familiar perfume and being delighted by it, Anna licked and licked, faster and faster in response to the excited and exciting moans that came from the girl on the bed. Her enthusiasm soared as Miranda writhed on the sheets, just as Anna had done moments before. Anna kept right on licking, now more confidently and harder, until Miranda's hands clutched at her head and she cried, 'I'm going to come!'

Up and down, Miranda's hips bucked, so that Anna felt as though her tongue was actually fucking the other girl. Then Miranda pushed Anna away from the centre of her pleasure and pulled her up on to the bed so that they were level and their mouths touched once more. Flipping Anna over on to her back with surprising strength, Miranda ground the mound of her pubis against Anna's, and they rocked backwards and forwards together, Miranda's hands grasping for Anna's breasts, Anna's hands sweeping up and down Miranda's back, twisting up fistfuls of her long blonde hair. Miranda was moaning, sighing, desperately clutching her lover's body to her own. Anna's mouth sought Miranda's hungrily. They kissed as though they were trying to devour one another.

Then Anna put just one finger into Miranda's vagina. The muscles hidden there were opening and closing in an ecstatic sine wave as Miranda soaked her lover's hand. 'I'm coming, I'm coming,' she continued to scream, as Anna pumped her finger in and out of the pulsing vagina.

She could hardly believe what she had just done.

Chapter Thirteen

The next morning, Anna lay awake on her bed long before Georgios got round to crowing his silly chicken head off. She looked at her watch lying on the bedside table. It was five-thirty. Then she looked askance at the girl on the bed beside her, sleeping quietly in the place that Anna's imagination had thus far reserved for Justin.

It was almost full light outside. Anna shook Miranda gently. The blonde girl smiled in her sleep and batted away an imaginary fly.

'Miranda,' Anna whispered urgently. 'It's time to get up. Miranda. Wake up!'

Miranda opened her sea-green eyes and rolled towards Anna. She had a contented smile on her face now. Anna didn't know what she had expected to see there. Shock, perhaps. Or embarrassment, as the memory of the previous night crept in and took hold.

'It's not time to go to work yet, is it?' Miranda whined, as if nothing out of the ordinary had happened. As if she woke up beside Anna every day . . .

'No,' said Anna, biting her lip. 'It's just that, I thought – under the circumstances . . . I thought it might be better if you weren't seen coming out of my room. You know what I mean. Vangelis will be up in half an hour and . . .'

'Ah, Vangelis,' Miranda said slyly. 'Now we're getting to the bottom of it. You're always so worried about what Vangelis thinks. You must be falling in love with him.'

Anna sighed. 'I'm not . . . You know why . . .'

'It's OK,' Miranda continued, putting a finger to Anna's lips to save her the explanation. 'I won't let you down.' Planting a quick kiss where her finger had been, she got up from the bed and began to look for the clothes she had discarded in such a hurry.

'No one will guess, Anna. Sex doesn't show on your face, you know. Whichever way you have it.' Miranda planted one last kiss on Anna's cheek and then she was gone. Anna's heart didn't stop racing, however, until she heard the sound of Miranda's door shutting safely behind her. Then panic set her off again. If she could hear Miranda closing her door and walking across her room, then surely the other people in the house would have heard everything that went on in the night. *Everything.*

Breakfast loomed like a lifetime in purgatory. Miranda might not say anything, but she would be certain to spend the whole day trying to make meaningful eye contact across the sand up at the dig. Anna covered her eyes with her hands. What was more, she had just been unfaithful to Justin – and with a girl. If he ever found out, she knew he would explode like a landmine, right in the middle of the trading floor.

But there was to be no avoiding Miranda. Or so Anna thought. When Georgios finally sounded the alarm, Anna dragged herself out of bed and headed for the shower. The warm water splashing on her skin seemed to reactivate the scents and even the sensations of the night before. Anna could smell the light flowery perfume that followed Miranda like a veil. Then a wave of the delicate warm musk that emanated from an aroused vagina . . . When she bent to wash between her legs, the tenderness that still lingered there reminded her mercilessly of how she had come to feel so raw.

Anna wanted to stand beneath the shower until she had washed her whole body down the plughole, but soon Dr Sillery was banging on the door, demanding to be allowed in to shave.

'What are you doing in there?' he shouted. 'Drowning?'

Anna slunk out of the shower wrapped in a towel, and avoided her boss's eyes as she passed.

'Not talking to me this morning then?' Dr Sillery asked sarcastically.

In the kitchen, Vangelis was already at the table. He didn't even look up when Anna walked into the room, but continued to butter toast messily while reading the latest archaeological journal just arrived from Athens. 'Morning,' he managed to mumble between mouthfuls.

Was he just being tactful? Anna wondered. She felt sure that everybody knew. It was as though she had grown horns overnight. She toyed with the idea of trying to provoke some kind of comment from Vangelis to ascertain exactly what he thought of her now.

'Didn't get much sleep last night,' she muttered.

'Yes. It was very hot,' said Vangelis flatly. 'It may be better tonight. There is going to be more wind from the sea today.'

There wasn't much she could read into that.

Finally, the breakfast ordeal was over. Dr Sillery announced that Miranda wouldn't be joining them that morning. She wasn't feeling too well apparently.

'Been up all night with her friends in the village,' Vangelis commented acidly.

'Do you think so?' Anna asked, feigning innocence.

'Yes. I don't suppose she came home until five o'clock in the morning.'

Anna nodded. He didn't know what had really happened. He obviously didn't know. But she still spent the day feeling like a rubber band that had been stretched to the limit.

She decided that she would have to tell her so recently acquired new lover that what had happened between them could never happen again. Miranda would get over it. It hadn't taken her long to get Vangelis out of her system. Anna agonised over the right words all day, but when they got back to the villa, Miranda wasn't there to be told. A note on the kitchen table announced that she had gone down to the village. Dr Sillery scrunched the paper up furiously.

'Huh! So she's well enough to go and visit her friends in the taverna, but not to come to work. I think that Miss Sharpe and I will have to have words when she finally gets back.'

Join the queue, thought Anna silently, though she was secretly relieved that Miranda seemed to be back to her usual tricks already.

Until dawn the next morning, when Anna woke from a hazy and fitful sleep, punctuated by a nasty dream about being chased by a bulldog, to find Miranda standing at the end of her bed. Wearing just a silky camisole, a pair of barely there lace knickers, and the smuggest grin Anna had ever seen.

'No,' was Anna's first word to her. Then, only slightly more patiently, 'What do you want?'

'Come into my room,' Miranda said urgently. 'I've got something amazing I want to show you.'

'I've already seen it,' said Anna.

'That's not very nice. But don't kid yourself that I want your body again this morning, Anna. It's far more exciting than that.'

'And you're waking me up at this godforsaken hour especially? This I have to see.' Anna dragged herself from her pillow and followed Miranda upstairs.

Once they were inside Miranda's room and the door was safely shut, Miranda reached under her bed and brought out something that had been carefully wrapped in tissue paper.

'What is it?' asked Anna. 'You had better have a good reason for interrupting my beauty sleep.'

'Good? It's fantastic. In fact, my personal opinion is that it's going to be the most important archaeological find this century.' Miranda smiled as she began to unwrap her precious bundle.

'Archaeological find? What do you mean? You weren't even at the dig today.'

'I picked it up in the village where Nicky lives,' Miranda explained. 'His brother is an artisan. And a most talented faker of art.'

Anna's lips twisted into a smile as Miranda shook the last of the paper free from an elegantly curved vase. 'Amazing, isn't it?' she said, holding it out for Anna to see. 'And absolutely disgraceful. Turn it round and have a look at what the minotaur is doing to the queen.'

Anna obliged. On the other side of the vase, a man with the oversized head of a fierce black bull was bending over a graceful Minoan lady and lifting up her skirts to do something completely unspeakable. 'That looks exciting,' Anna mused. 'But what are you going to do with this, Miranda? Old Sillery will know that it's not the real thing as soon as he sees it.'

'I wouldn't be so sure. I'm going to bury it somewhere on the site. After I've chipped a bit off here and there for luck and rubbed a handful or two of dirt all over it for that genuine aged effect, of course . . . He's not going to think that it's a fake if he finds it in the right place, is he? At least, not at first. And hopefully not until he's crowed his silly head off about his valuable find at some big symposium. I just want to see him get overexcited for a while. If we're really lucky, he might even cream his pants.'

'I'm not having anything to do with this. You're already deeply into his bad books.'

'Am I?'

'After you skived off yesterday to go into the village, you are.'

'This will cheer him up.'

'Are you mad? He'll go insane if he finds out what you're doing now,' said Anna, carefully putting the vase back down on Miranda's bed.

'But you won't tell him, will you?' Miranda asked seriously. 'I've waited a long time for this.'

'Of course I won't tell him. While I don't want to be in on this frankly totally fault-ridden scheme of yours, I'd secretly quite like to see you try to get away with it.'

'Good. I'll get started right away.' Miranda took a little hammer from her desk and started to tap gently around the area where the minotaur was ploughing none too delicately into the swooning queen. Eventually, their locked genitals came away in one perfect piece.

'Stylish' murmured Anna.

'I like to think so.'

*   *   *

Since hearing of Miranda's plot, Anna had been on tenterhooks waiting to see it put into action. She had expected Miranda to bury the vase at the site straight away, to save herself the bother of being in trouble about the skive, but Miranda simply took her ticking-off like a trooper instead. When nothing happened after a week, Anna was almost starting to think that Miranda had thought better of her scheme.

But then Dr Sillery suddenly whooped with joy from the opposite end of the dig and began to dance around like someone who has just won the lottery. Or been bitten by a wasp. He had found something truly fantastic, he yelled. Miranda and Anna looked up from their respective jobs and shared a knowing glance.

'Is this it?' Anna asked.

'I'm sure I don't know what you're talking about,' said Miranda with a smile. 'But I think it might be. Vengeance is mine, as they say.'

Downing tools, they followed Vangelis, and the two young Greek students who had been drafted in to help get things moving more quickly, up the hill to where Dr Sillery stood, staring at the ground in what appeared to be a state of rapture. It was either that or catatonic paralysis.

'What have you found?' Miranda asked innocently.

'I'm not sure,' said Dr Sillery breathlessly. 'But I think it may be the greatest Minoan find since the palace at Knossos. Look. Here.' He pointed at a shard of pottery which still lay embedded in the ground. 'Someone take reference photos of the position of this piece quickly. I want to dig it out right away and be sure.'

'Just looks like part of a vase to me,' said Vangelis.

'Exactly. But look at the subject matter, people. Have you ever seen anything quite like this before?'

Anna and Miranda pretended to be as surprised by the shard painted with genitals as Dr Sillery was. 'Wow, that's a bit hot,' said Anna, recognising the scene.

'It is. It is. I can't wait to find the rest of the vase.'

Vangelis took the reference photos as quickly as he could. As soon as Vangelis had finished, Dr Sillery fell to his knees in the dirt and began to scrabble around the little piece of pottery feverishly. It wasn't long before he found what he was hoping for. Vangelis took reference pictures again and pretty soon, Dr Sillery was lifting Miranda's vase above his head as though it was the UEFA Cup.

'Incredible,' he murmured. 'Look. It's absolutely perfect but for this single hole. And the shard I found first obviously fits the hole exactly. Amazing. Perhaps they knocked this piece out for decency's sake.'

'What's the rest of the picture?' asked Vangelis innocently.

'It seems to be the minotaur. Yes, a minotaur and a Minoan queen. Having anal sex, I think.'

Miranda shared a dirty smile with Anna.

'Oh, happy day,' Dr Sillery continued. 'To have found this. I can't believe my luck. I must phone Professor Horowitz straight away.'

'Do you think you should?' asked Anna nervously. Miranda gave her a sharp dig in the ribs.

'Why, yes. Don't you see that this find suggests that we could be standing on the most important archaeological site found in decades?'

'But don't you think you ought to wait until we're a little clearer as to exactly what we're dealing with?' Anna continued. 'After all, you know Professor Horowitz as well as I do, Dr Sillery. One sniff of glory and he'll be all over the place, perhaps even claiming that he dug the vase up himself. If you do the research work surrounding the vase first, it will make it that much harder for him to take over the show when he finds out.'

'Mmm,' said Dr Sillery, stroking his chin. 'I think perhaps you're right. Well done.'

Anna grinned with relief, while Miranda's face was clouded with fury.

'Right, everybody. I'm much too excited to stay out here,' Dr Sillery announced next. 'I'm going back to my room to do some reading around this incredible new piece and you people can pack up in two hours' time as a special treat. What do you say we have a bit of a celebration tonight?'

Everyone agreed that was the best idea Dr Sillery had ever had, and once he had vanished back to his ivory tower with the vase carefully laid in a sand-box, everyone soon forgot about another two hours' work and downed tools anyway.

'Well, he certainly seems to have fallen for it,' Anna commented, while she and Miranda shared a cigarette behind the cataloguing tent. 'Unbelievable.'

'Yeah. But what are you trying to do, telling him not to ring Horowitz? You're ruining the plan.'

'I just don't think you should let it go too far. If, or should I say when, Professor Horowitz finds out that that vase of yours is a fake, poor old William will be laughed out of the archaeological community.'

'Huh,' sniffed Miranda. 'That was the idea. And it won't be as if he doesn't deserve it. We can pack up in two hours, indeed. That's the time we usually down tools anyway.'

'Oh, stop moaning. We're going to have a cele-bration tonight.'

'Yes, and what will that be?' asked Miranda bitterly. 'Extra milk and biscuits before we go to bed?'

Chapter Fourteen

Luckily, Dr Sillery put Vangelis in charge of getting in the supplies.

'What is this stuff?' Sillery sniffed the colourless, yet strangely viscous liquid in the tiny glass cup suspiciously.

'It is raki,' Vangelis explained. 'The local speciality. You can knock it straight back in one or sip it slowly if you like. But the one rule is that you have to drink it with friends.' He poured out glasses for Anna and Miranda as well. '*Yamas,*' he said, raising his glass in a toast. 'Here's to the new Knossos.'

'The new Knossos,' the others replied, with Miranda trying hard not to laugh out loud.

After the toast, Anna and Miranda, old hands at the raki business by now, sipped carefully at the little glasses as though the liquid might be poison, but Sillery knocked his straight back like a fool. Miranda raised her eyebrows at the sight of the venerable academic being so rash.

'Fill 'er up, Vangelis,' the doctor said, slamming his glass on the table.

Vangelis obliged happily and pretty soon Sillery had downed three glasses of the lethal liquid while the girls were still cautiously dealing with their first. His cheeks were already beginning to glow.

'I can't tell you,' he said, after his eighth little glass of the poison, 'how much it means to me to have made this incredible discovery here today. Especially,' he sniffed, 'especially after the terrible time I've been through lately. I thought that I had nothing left to live for. But now, now I have everything to live for. I can't thank you people enough for all your hard work and help with this discovery.'

Miranda took the thanks graciously. Anna blushed and stared into her glass. 'You're going to have to let him know the truth before he gives us all a raise. Are you going to tell him tonight?' she hissed into Miranda's ear, after Dr Sillery had downed his twentieth raki and was promising to write them all into his will.

'Nah, he's happy,' Miranda replied.

'At the moment, yes. But haven't you ever heard that phrase "the harder they fall"? If he takes his discovery to the outside world and they let him know that it is a fake, it'll kill him. He's obviously been on the edge for weeks as it is.'

'You're overreacting.'

'I don't think so. But he certainly is.'

'I'll tell him before it goes too far. I promise. Just let me have my fun first.'

'There are jokes and jokes, Miranda. And I don't think he'll ever see the funny side of this one.'

'Why don't you tell him yourself if you're so concerned?'

'Because the messenger always gets shot.'

'What are you two lovely ladies whispering about?' Dr Sillery asked. They both squeaked, 'Nothing!'

'Good,' he said. 'Then have another glass of this delicious drink.'

But two hours later, at Anna's insistence, Miranda grudgingly took off her high-heeled sandals and picked her way across the stony path to the site where Dr Sillery was standing, swaying very slightly from the raki, and smiling broadly at the starry sky as if he were suddenly sure of the existence of a beneficent god. Then he heard Miranda creep up behind him, and turned to apply his broad smile to her instead.

'Look at all those stars,' he murmured dreamily. 'And just think: every single one of those little stars is the equivalent of our own beloved sun. If only we could get as far as the planets that circle those other suns, imagine what incredible riches of history we might find hidden there.'

'Mmm.' Miranda nodded.

'It is the most amazing thing, Miranda,' Sillery said, suddenly taking hold of her hands, 'to be privileged to look into the lives of these ancient people long after they are dead and then to find that we have so much in common with those who went before. I mean, I bet that before you saw that vase I found this afternoon, you assumed that all Minoan children were conceived via immaculate conception.'

'Mmm,' said Miranda, picking a stone out from between her toes. 'Not quite.'

'But now we have proof that the Minoans were probably even more open about sex than we people in the modern world are today. Unequivocal proof. Imagine entertaining your grandmother with a teapot depicting anal intercourse between a woman and a mythical beast,' he mused.

'Mmm. I think I'd rather not. Listen, Dr Sillery . . .'

'Oh, call me William, Miranda, please.'

'OK. Listen, William.' It seemed strange, not referring to him as the Doctor. 'It's about that vase that I'd like to talk to you, if you've got a moment to spare . . .'

'Of course I have. I'm all ears now.'

Miranda made him sit down on the wall beside her, still holding on to his hand tightly. She took a deep breath and prepared to confess all. She had to. As Anna wouldn't let her forget, it was the only thing to do. The decent thing. Then she exhaled again. The words were still unspoken. William looked at her expectantly. His previously sour face had been utterly transfigured by the elation of his discovery. Smiling as he was now, he might even be considered quite handsome.

Miranda smiled back, her own grin stiff with strain. At this rate, her confession was never going to pass her throat.

William squeezed her hand and spoke for her. 'Look, I know you think I've been pretty hard on you all these past few weeks, Miranda, but just think, if I hadn't pushed you to work so quickly, we might never have found the vase. It might have been smashed into a million pieces in the foundations of the new hotel. I promise you that none of my harsh words were meant to hurt you or make you feel stupid. I'm just passionate about history. Absolutely passionate about it. That's all.'

Miranda continued to smile. William's eyes were twinkling like merry little stars in the light of the lamp he had brought out to the site. It was becoming increasingly clear to Miranda that Anna had been right. She was looking at a man with a dream, and her prank, if it wasn't stopped in time, could destroy him. Miranda had a horrible premonition of this gentle man being laughed out of a university lecture hall by some of the finest brains in the world. But then she thought of Adam.

She thought of her beautiful, beloved Adam, telling her that he couldn't see her again because someone had threatened to tell his wife about her. Dr William Sillery was the only person who knew about their affair. He had seen its tentative beginnings during last year's dig in Crete and therefore it stood to reason that he was the man responsible for the abrupt end to Miranda's happiness. Now she had the chance for revenge.

'You were going to tell me something,' he said. 'But I interrupted you. What was it?'

He was so calm, so serene, so happy. Miranda held his life in her hands. She wasn't going to let him off lightly yet.

'About the vase?' William persisted.

'Oh, yes. I was wondering if you thought it might have been used in some kind of erotic ritual,' she bluffed quickly.

William settled back in his place on the wall, with a look of surprise. 'Well,' he laughed, slightly nervously. 'I don't honestly know. I suppose that is a possibility.' He folded his arms while he thought about the question. Against her better judgement, Miranda couldn't help but admire the knotted muscle acquired over years of shifting stone. 'Maybe it did have a special purpose to those ends.'

William licked his lips, making them glisten invitingly above his square, stubbly chin. He pushed his glasses up on his nose, then took them off altogether. Without their unflattering frames to hide his chiselled face, he really could have been an Indiana Jones.

'What made you ask me that?' he questioned her, staring hard into her eyes.

'It's just that . . .' Miranda fumbled for a reason. Was he staring at her with intent? Or was he staring just because he had taken off his glasses? 'It's just that,' she stuttered, 'I don't really know if I should say this . . . It's just that ever since the vase was discovered this afternoon, I've been feeling strangely stirred, deep inside. Strangely aroused, I suppose. It's almost as if some ancient erotic power is still resonating within the pottery.'

William nodded slowly. 'This sounds fascinating. Carry on, my dear. Carry on.'

'And it's as if that power, from the vase I mean, has been resonating inside me tonight,' Miranda continued, almost enjoying herself now as she watched another smile spread across William's normally straight thin lips. 'You know, I think I can feel some kind of tingling at my very core. A crying out for the missing piece that will complete the picture.' She pointed towards her stomach in illustration.

'Ah-ha, like the piece of the vase that was broken away.'

'Yes, that's right. Exactly. Exactly like that.'

'I think I know what you mean, Miranda. It could certainly be a metaphor for my current emotional position.'

'Do you feel like there's something missing from your life too?' Miranda asked as sincerely as she could manage.

William locked his eyes on hers. There was no way he could answer that question with words. Miranda squirmed beneath *his* gaze and found to her surprise that she was breathing much more quickly than usual as she looked back at him now. In fact, her chest was almost fluttering with anticipation. She found she simply couldn't take her gaze from his challenging grey eyes.

'Perhaps we should do something about it,' he murmured suddenly.

Miranda almost fell off the wall in shock. Never had she heard William Sillery sound like that. So determined. So masculine. So attractive. While she was getting over the shock, he moved in for the clinch.

'Oh, William,' she squeaked, as he covered her soft mouth with his and tipped her backwards in his arms.

'Miranda! I've waited so long for this moment,' he murmured in reply.

Almost without thinking, William shrugged off his shirt and laid it on the hard ground beside them. Then, taking Miranda firmly in his arms, he lifted her from the wall and set her down on top of the shirt.

'Won't this interfere with our professional relationship?' Miranda asked nervously, as William showered kisses upon her face.

'No. I promise we'll have finished before I need you to start work in the morning,' he said, without a hint of a laugh.

William's hands were soon beneath her tight white T-shirt, sliding over her warm brown skin in the direction of her pillowy breasts. Miranda couldn't help arching her back as his fingers found her nipples, clearly defined against her breasts even through the thick lace of her expensive bra. William pushed the lace of one cup aside and rolled the little pink nipple bud between his fingers until it could harden no more. Then his hands slipped around to Miranda's back and sought out the clasp. The clasp sprang open as if by magic. He began to push Miranda's T-shirt up over her head. Her bra followed, and soon she was naked from the waist up.

William continued to kiss her ardently as he fondled the twin orbs he had just released. Miranda allowed him to take control, probing her mouth with his tongue, even gently biting her full lips between his sharp white teeth. William too was naked now but for his shorts. Miranda let her hands wander over his broad, bronzed shoulders, then down over his chest, where a cloud of springy dark hair covered a surprisingly fine, firm pair of pectoral muscles.

By the time William finally got round to kissing her breasts, Miranda was moving on to the buckle of his belt. The soft, worn brown leather slipped easily from the silver buckle. Then she popped open the button at the top of his flies. The zip slid down easily, too, and Miranda soon had her hand inside, delighted to discover that William was wearing no underpants, when his warm shaft throbbed powerfully beneath her palm.

While she gently stroked William's penis into hardness, he was carelessly unfastening her shorts and sliding them down over her knees. His work-roughened hand sought out the spicy warmth between her legs, and his long strong fingers, which Miranda had often secretly admired while watching him cataloguing artefacts, began to probe inside.

Miranda felt her clitoris spring to attention as William carefully worked at it with the heel of his hand, his fingers stroking the wetness of her vagina. In her delicate grasp, his penis, too, was reaching top capacity. It was as hard as some ancient fertility symbol hewn from marble, and Miranda longed to put it to good use.

Wriggling completely free of her shorts at last, Miranda positioned herself so that she was directly under William and brought her long legs up on either side of his body. The message that she sent to him now was unequivocal, and he soon turned his attention from massaging her clitoris to the business of entering her. Miranda was almost breathless with excitement, with the thrill of it all. Here she was, seducing her boss, seducing her nemesis, Dr William Sillery: artefact fiend, ice king. His thick hot shaft nudged at her labia, begging to be allowed in. Miranda slipped her hand down between her legs to part the lips that were barring William's entrance, then carefully guided him inside.

In the flattering caress of the moonlight, years dropped away from William's face as he began to make love to Miranda. She had never seen him look so young, so handsome, so determined. She pulled his face down towards hers, overcome with the desire to kiss his full, smooth lips again. Her hands roamed all over the soft skin of his back, right to the downy cleft in his buttocks.

Their love-making was as frantic and frenzied as only the love-making of two people who have unknowingly desired each other for so long can be. Miranda felt transformed into some kind of mythical animal as they rutted beneath the canopy of stars as though their sex was part of an ancient ritual. With his teeth gritted in determination as he rode her, William was like a centaur, roughly stealing the virginity of some young maiden, first favoured, but then abandoned by the gods.

As she lay on the floor beneath her lover, Miranda felt as though she could actually feel the ancient earth spinning on its axis. The stars sailed above them in a celestial light-show that reflected the electricity passing between their two bodies locked in lust. Miranda grasped William tightly to her breast, biting his ear as he hammered his body against hers. Within her, her heart seemed to have become a core of molten lava. The chilly breeze from the sea could no longer keep her body cool as she neared the climax of her life.

William, too, was experiencing something of an epiphany. The animal passions he had kept so carefully reined in during his long and loveless marriage were battling to be free. As he rammed his shaft hard into Miranda, he bit at the soft golden skin of her neck. She responded by scratching her sharp fingernails down his back. The pain only made him work harder.

As the end of their sudden and unexpected tryst grew near, their moans and groans and sharply inhaled breaths echoed loudly around the hillside. Miranda looked up at the stars once more but could no longer get a focus. Her concentration was being directed elsewhere. She made one last grab for William's buttocks, as she felt his shaft harden and swell against the roof of her vagina. For her own part, she felt weightless, despite the bulk of the perfect body that lay on top of hers. It was as if she had left her flesh behind and was experiencing her orgasm on a far higher plain.

'William,' she called out, 'William . . . don't stop, please!'

Back at the villa, Vangelis and Anna sat alone at last on the patio. The student helpers were long gone. Why sit up talking archaeology when the clubs in town were still open? Vangelis poured out a final glass of raki for himself. Anna covered her little cup when he tried to pour some out for her.

'I'll only regret it in the morning,' she told him.

At that moment, they heard a loud, ecstatic cry from the direction of the site.

'Do you think they'll regret that in the morning, too?' Vangelis laughed.

Anna looked down at the table, suddenly shy. When she looked up again, Vangelis still had his eyes fixed on her. It was the first time they had been properly alone since that nasty disagreement over breakfast.

'Does she like him?' Vangelis asked.

'What?' Anna felt strangely hot under Vangelis's gaze. She pulled the collar of her shirt away from her clammy neck and flapped it about for some air.

'I mean Miranda. Does she really like Dr Sillery?'

'Sounds like it,' Anna said, referring to the shrieks still echoing around the hills. 'Though I think perhaps it's rather the case that she thinks she owes him one.'

'Owes him one?' Vangelis repeated curiously. 'You'll have to explain that to me.'

'I mean, she feels guilty about something. So she's trying to make up for it.'

'What does she have to feel guilty about?' Vangelis asked innocently.

Anna knew she was getting dangerously close to confessing Miranda's hair-brain plan, and she wasn't quite sure that Vangelis would approve. 'I don't know. For being so moody with him ever since we got here, I suppose. It's her way of saying that she wants to be his friend.'

'She has a very strange way of making friends,' mused Vangelis. Then he fixed Anna with his gorgeous gaze again and asked provocatively, 'Do you want to be my friend?'

Anna snorted. 'We're already friends, Vangelis.'

'Yes,' said Vangelis softly. 'That's what we are.'

There was a moment of silence between them – while Anna wondered if she was meant to read anything into his words. Or whether she wanted to. Just as the breakdown in the conversation was getting to be unbearable, Vangelis stood up and gathered together the little glasses.

'I'll see you in the morning,' he told her flatly.

'Yeah,' said Anna. 'See you then.'

She watched him go, then stared back out into the darkness in the direction of the sea. She could see the lights of a little boat being rocked by the waves. She wondered if it was Nicky's boat. She wondered who was on board with him tonight. Miranda's tinkling laughter, echoing down from the site, suggested that she didn't much care who Nicky was with. Anna wavered between thinking Miranda foolish or just free-spirited. She wasn't letting the man she had left behind hold her back when it came to satisfying her primeval urges. Was she lonely or lucky? And should Anna be doing the same?

Chapter Fifteen

'Well? Did you tell him?' Anna asked her wayward friend the next morning.

Miranda drew her shoulders up towards her head in a cringe. 'I couldn't, Anna. I tried to, I promise. But he was way too happy about the whole thing. He wouldn't stop going on about it. That vase has transformed him.'

'So I heard,' said Anna somewhat sarcastically. 'But I was serious when I told you what might happen if you let him carry on believing . . .'

'I know, I know,' Miranda snapped. 'I promise I'll sort something out.'

'Like what?'

'Just leave it with me, will you?' she almost shouted. Then, in an unaccustomed show of sulkiness, Miranda flounced out into the garden.

She was confused. Dr William Sillery, the bane of her life, had suddenly become her lover. Where did that leave her? Did she owe him her loyalty now? Did she owe him the truth about the vase? Or was he only going to get what he deserved for ruining her life when the truth came out at some symposium?

Miranda lit up a cigarette and looked out across the churning sea. In the distance, she could see a small boat bobbing on the waves. Was it Nicky? she wondered. Taking some other girl for a ride? Miranda didn't really care. Nicky meant nothing to her. He was just one of a veritable parade of well-hung young men who had passed through her love life, leaving behind only the faintest impression on her memory. Perhaps more if they had driven a good car. Unlike Adam. Since arriving in Crete it had slowly dawned on Miranda that Anna had been right. Her affair with Adam really had affected her far more than she was prepared to admit. In fact, the painful truth was that Adam was the only man she had ever loved.

And because he had pushed them apart, she decided, William Sillery deserved to be punished. Let him find out the truth about the vase the hard way. Miranda wanted him to fall in love with his bloody inanimate discovery and feel the pain of having the thing he treasured most ripped away. As for having slept with him, perhaps that wasn't so much at odds with her plan, she decided. Perhaps that extra betrayal would make the pain of the vase even harder to bear. Miranda nodded to herself in resolution. But she still didn't feel happy.

Suddenly she felt a hand on her shoulder.

'I'm sorry I keep pushing you to tell him.'

It was Anna.

'But I feel like you've both become my friends lately. I don't want to see either of you hurt. And if this goes on too long William might not be the only one with egg on his face, you know.'

Miranda nodded. She knew that William wouldn't be the only one whose reputation bit the dust if the whole thing came out, but a life without archaeology could be no worse than a life without Adam.

'I'll tell him if you like,' Anna continued. 'I'll get him to let me take a proper look at the vase and suggest that it might not be the real thing. I won't even hint at why I know it isn't.'

'Thanks. But I don't need you to do that. I'll deal with this myself.'

'I think he's in his bedroom now,' said Anna, hoping that Miranda would seize the moment to make amends while she was in a vaguely sensible state of mind.

Miranda smiled and said that she would go and see him right away. Moments later, Anna saw William draw shut the curtains of his bedroom, which was next to her own on the ground floor. If Miranda had let him know the truth it must have gone well, since it looked as though they were already kissing and making up. Silently, Anna crept to the window and put her eye to the gap in the curtains. She longed to know what was being said.

Inside the bedroom, Miranda was sitting on the edge of William's desk, her long brown legs crossed seductively at the knee.

'I should be getting some work done,' said William, tidying up his tie. 'I only came in to get cleaned up.'

'It's Sunday,' said Miranda.

'Yes, but I'm planning to call Professor Horowitz tomorrow morning. I'm itching to let him know about the vase.'

'I'd love to be with you when you make the call,' Miranda purred.

'I was thinking of inviting him out here, actually. Showing him the find in situ. More impressive like that.'

Outside the window, Anna clapped her hand to her forehead in despair. If Professor Horowitz came out to Crete and pronounced the vase a fake, the revelation would reflect on all of them, not just William, and Anna didn't want the world authority on Minoan culture to think that she didn't know a real artefact from her asshole. Her career was at stake too. She was going to have to resolve the matter herself.

Meanwhile, Miranda got up from the desk and was now sitting astride William in his chair. She was unbuttoning the crisp white shirt he had only just put on and tracing a pattern in the hair on his chest.

'Still feeling the power of the vase?' she asked him, as the beginnings of a hard-on twitched at the front of his trousers. William pushed back his fringe from his forehead.

'I've certainly been feeling warm today, but I thought it was just the weather.'

Miranda laughed her tinkling laugh. She loved the way that William acted so naive, until the right buttons were pushed. She leaned forward and bit the side of his neck affectionately. She felt his fingers dig into the fleshy curves of her buttocks as she kissed him, and knew then for certain that he wouldn't get much work done that afternoon.

'There's still something missing deep inside me,' said Miranda lasciviously as she popped the last button on William's shirt and pushed it from his shoulders. She nuzzled his bare collarbone and gently bit at his ear lobe. William closed his eyes in a last futile gesture of resistance, then slid his own hands slowly beneath the hem of Miranda's flowery skirt.

Her skin was as smooth as the cold flesh of a perfect marble Venus. When William leaned his face into the side of her neck, he could smell summer meadows, beautiful flowers. All the beautiful scents of an English countryside. But beneath the innocence was a hint of danger. Musk. A hint of arousal. He breathed her in deeply and felt the smell of her seductive femininity permeate his very loins.

'You can tell me to go if you want to. If you want to get on with your work,' she said almost childishly, as she fumbled with the button at the waistband of his trousers. His scent was equally arousing to her. She breathed in deeply and let herself be filled with the fresh smell of laundry, underpinned by the spicy tang of masculine sweat. She couldn't understand how she had worked so close by William for such a long time and not noticed how delicious he was before.

William didn't answer her with words. Instead he fastened his mouth on hers and kissed her as though he were trying to suck out her breath. His hands felt cold on her warm back as he sought out the clasp on her bra. Miranda sighed when he unfastened it, delighting in the feeling of her heavy breasts swinging free.

'Let's lie down,' she whispered, leading him towards the unmade bed. She lay down first, throwing her arms above her head so that her dress rode up her thighs, revealing acres of soft bronzed flesh. William stood at the bottom of the bed, shaking off his shirt sleeves and pushing down his newly ironed trousers over his own stone-hard thighs.

Miranda shuddered with anticipation at the sight of his nearly naked body. Keeping his soft grey cotton pants on, he got on to the bed and crawled towards her. Miranda pulled him down on top of her, kissing him hungrily as she worked his pants down past his buttocks, eager to relish the hard-on that held the pants out like a tent in front.

'I want you,' she breathed hotly as William pulled up her dress and covered her flat belly with butterfly kisses. His fingers tangled in her pubic hair and Miranda began to feel that familiar hot wetness creeping out of her vagina and on to her silky inner thighs. William's breathing was urgent as he rubbed at her clitoris, but Miranda didn't need much foreplay, she just needed him inside.

Opening her legs a little wider, Miranda encouraged William on top of her. She held his buttocks as he guided himself inside her and bit her lip when she felt the glorious completeness of the first tender thrust.

Starting off slowly, William undulated his pelvis against Miranda's with glorious precision. Every stroke seemed to hit her G-spot and soon her body was humming inside. Miranda slid her hands up and down his back, first stroking, then scratching, making William throw back his head in painful delight.

'I'm going to come,' he warned her quickly, but Miranda wasn't ready for the game to be over so soon. Taking his penis firmly by its base, she made him withdraw, then flipped him over on to his back so that the shaft twitched straight up at the ceiling. Next Miranda straddled him, her knees on either side of his youthful narrow pelvis. She lowered herself down upon him with a groan of heartfelt rapture.

Tightening her thigh muscles she started to move herself slowly up and down. It was delicious, being able to control the speed and depth of his thrusts so completely. She had only to decide when she wanted to come to make it happen. Below her, William seemed to have been transported to some far off place on a wave of ecstasy. His hands gently caressed her buttocks as she moved, but he didn't dare interfere with the pace, which was, in any case, just perfect.

Soon he found his orgasm had crept up on him again and his stomach muscles contracted slightly as he tried to hold the explosion inside. He opened his eyes to see Miranda like a vision, a land-bound mermaid. Her blonde hair floated around her face and shoulders like a halo. She looked otherworldly, perfect. Her white teeth glistened as she parted her red lips to smile down on him like a goddess.

'Oh, oh,' she sighed, as she increased the speed of her movements little by little until she reached the point of no turning back. William wasn't alone in struggling to hold back his climax. Miranda's air of control began to slip away from her as she rode his cock more urgently. She reached a hand behind her to stroke his swollen balls. Her vagina was electrified with sensation, and her thighs began to shake with each laboured movement. Then, almost without warning she threw herself forward to cover William's face with kisses as she came and came and came.

Holding her breath so that she didn't make the slightest sound, Anna crept away from William's window mere seconds before the climax. She hadn't meant to watch for as long as she did, but the incredible passion between her colleagues had drawn her in like some magical magnet. However, apart from the fact that she didn't want to be caught standing outside if William decided to throw open the curtains to get some post-coital air, Anna had suddenly come up with the perfect way to end the vase dilemma and she needed William to be totally distracted while she put her plan into action. Seeing him with his eyes tightly shut as he hurtled towards a tremendous orgasm, Anna realised that she was seeing William as distracted as he was ever going to be, and headed for the makeshift office where the vase lay unguarded in all its splendour.

Two hours later, a blood-curdling scream from the direction of the office gave Miranda the first clue that something was going on.

'It's gone! It's gone! The vase has gone,' William yelled as he raced out on to the verandah. 'Call the police!' he was shouting now. 'Call the United Nations! Call anyone! Someone. Quickly. Someone help!'

Anna gave Miranda a knowing glance before she too rushed in to help look for the missing relic.

'Where on earth could it have gone?' asked Miranda, not knowing whether to be relieved or frustrated by the unexpected turn in events.

'Let's just say your fairy godmother spirited it away for your own good,' hissed Anna.

'You mean to say you took it?' Miranda whispered.

'Someone had to. He was going to ask Professor Horowitz to fly out here to see it tomorrow.'

'How do you know?' asked Miranda. Anna just shrugged, her face reddening slightly as she suddenly remembered where she had heard that particular plan. Meanwhile William was turning the house over, gnashing his teeth and pulling at his hair when none of the obvious hiding places revealed his precious vase.

'I don't know whether to thank you or kill you,' Miranda continued *sotto voce* beneath William's shouts.

'Well, don't bother repaying me in kind,' Anna smiled.

'It's useless,' William sobbed when he rejoined the girls in the office. 'The vase isn't in the house. It's been stolen. It's probably on its way to some antique dealer in Athens this very minute. But how could they have known that we had found something so valuable? Where's Vangelis?' he asked suddenly Their host hadn't been seen since breakfast. Realising the implications that were being drawn in William's mind, Anna shook her head.

'Now don't jump to conclusions, William. Vangelis said he was going to visit his grandmother today.'

'Defending lover-boy?' Miranda murmured with a smile.

Anna flashed a smile back and said through gritted teeth, 'Hadn't you better be taking someone to the police station?'

'We will find the thief,' William said sadly as he got into the jeep beside Miranda. 'And at least we still have the photographs Vangelis took and the drawings that Miranda made last night to help us. I just can't believe it, though. Why that vase? It can only be because they realised, as I did, that it was such an important find. They're obviously professionals, but we'll track the buggers down. They won't be able to sell it . . .'

Miranda slipped an arm around William's shoulders comfortingly and exhaled a sigh of relief in Anna's direction.

Anna merely raised an eyebrow.

Chapter Sixteen

But the Sunday night trip to the police station proved fairly useless. No one on duty could speak English, so the next morning, William set off to explain the whole thing again to the Chief of Police himself. Miranda went with him. It was the least she could do. (Not to mention the fact that Heraklion was the nearest thing to a shopping mecca Miranda was going to find on that tiny island.) Anna excused herself from the trip on the pretence of finishing some paperwork.

It wasn't entirely untrue. She had been away from England for five weeks now and there had been not one email, text or phone call from Justin to let her know where she stood in his affections, even after the erotic note she had sent to rekindle their relationship in his imagination. Now Anna wanted to spend the afternoon sorting the current position out in her head. She retired to her room with a sheaf of paper and a pen and tried to start a very different letter to Justin half a dozen times.

An hour later, six screwed up paper balls lay around the bin. She hadn't been a good enough aim to get them all inside. She had been trying to write a letter saying, 'I take it that things are over between us', but something was holding back the words. Quite what, she wasn't sure. It wasn't even as though she had actually missed him that much lately. When she was up at the dig, Anna thought of little but the artefacts she was sketching and in the evenings the lively debate around the dinner table kept her mind off the subject of home.

Home. That was the problem. The end of the dig loomed. Within a fortnight, she would be back in dirty old Camden Town. Right now, she felt almost as scared as she had been when she left Gatwick for Heraklion. Things would be different in Camden now. At least they would be if she and Justin were no longer together. It slowly dawned on Anna that Justin was the only reason she had stayed in London for three long grubby years as it was. Though she had never mentioned it to him, she had been aching to quit the city for the countryside for about two and a half of those three years. If Justin didn't want to see her any more, then there was no reason why she shouldn't end the lease on her cramped ugly flat and do exactly as she had dreamed.

Anna hugged her knees and looked out through her window on to the sea. She could even get a place by the ocean. A white painted cottage with huge bay windows that opened directly on to the beach. That would be nice. But the thought of the opportunities that would be reopened to her if she ended her relationship didn't quite take away the sting of its ending. Funny how the thought of being able to do exactly as you please doesn't always seem such a wonderful prospect . . .

She picked up her pen once more. 'Dear Justin, I think I . . .' Then she put the pen down, far too wound up now to write anything sensible. What she needed was to clear her head of everything but the salient points she wanted to deal with, and what better way to clear her head, she decided, than by taking a walk? Abandoning her half-written letter, she slipped on her sandals and headed out into the sun.

Anna had been walking for about half an hour when she saw a trampled path through the long grass and decided to cut away from the road. She had only walked a few metres down that path before she stopped to stare at the view. The sea had always been present as a wishy-washy blue horizon at the corner of her eye as she walked, but now she looked down at the shore and saw, instead of the usual collection of rocks and debris washed in by the tide, the most wonderful sandy beach hidden in a deep-sided cove. She stared and smiled, exhilarated to discover that the path she had chosen wove down to this gorgeous little beach and that she alone was there to make use of it. But at the same time she was a little sad, because half the joy of a beautiful view comes in sharing it, in being able to recall the memory of a sunny day with someone you love years down the line in front of a cold December night's fire.

Still, Anna decided that she was going to make the most of her find. She picked her way down the cliffside, following the footsteps of someone who had been there maybe a few weeks before, until finally she could forget about thinking where she should put her feet, and hit the soft sand. She slipped off her sandals and immediately the sun-warmed grains of gold began to burn her feet, forcing her to drop her little blue bag and skip to the edge of the water where the sand was damp and cool.

The sea that lapped at her toes was as clear and blue as the water on postcards from the Caribbean. Little sand-coloured fish darted in and out of the shallows, quite invisible until they suddenly moved in unison like a curtain of silvery shivers. When she stepped into the water, Anna was surprised to find that it really was as warm as a bath. At least it was as warm as the tepid, solar-heated bath back at the villa.

Suddenly feeling the need to be in right up to her neck in the glittering blue, Anna threw her baseball cap in the direction of her discarded bag. Thereafter followed her T-shirt and her shorts, until she stood once more at the edge of the water dressed only in a pair of soft white cotton pants. Her bikini was in her bag, but she decided that there was no reason to bother changing into it. She was, after all, the only person about for miles. As far as she could see, there was no one to mind if she didn't have a top on. So she waded in, until the waves began to lap at her waist, turning the little pants transparent so that she could see her pubic hair beneath.

After standing like this for a while, she decided that the only thing to do now was to throw herself right in. She lunged forward, letting the waves cover her body, relaxing as she welcomed their warm embrace.

Sighing with pleasure, she rolled over on to her back and made a star shape with her arms and legs. Like that, she could have floated for hours, letting the sun beat down on her face, while the sea gently rocked her like a lover. A seabird circled above, calling out tunelessly to its distant mate. Justin would love this, Anna suddenly thought. But as the picture of him reappeared in her mind, she started to feel quite cold. She started to swim briskly to fight off the creeping chill.

About ten minutes later, Anna was too cold to stay in the sea. She strode back up the beach, growing increasingly concerned as she drew nearer to the spot where she had left her bag. She prayed she wasn't right, but suddenly knew she had to be. The bag was nowhere to be seen. It must have been taken. But by whom?

Anna wrapped her arms around her body in a desperate attempt to keep warm as she scanned the beach for the culprit. But it wasn't just the water drying on her body that was making her feel cold. Until that moment, she had been sure that she was alone and the slowly dawning thought that someone had followed her down to this secret cove and taken her bag was of no comfort at all.

Eventually, she decided that she had no choice but to head back for the villa dressed as she was. It would be getting dark soon and it was difficult enough to cross that coastal path with shoes on in the daylight. She dreaded reaching the top of the slope, seeing the cars and buses thundering past on a road that was barely wide enough for a pedestrian. Would anyone stop to give nearly naked Englishwoman a lift? More to the point, would she want to risk taking a lift with the kind of person who might offer one?

Anna was almost ready to cry when she saw the blue plastic bag tangled in the thorny branches of a nearby bush. She plucked it free, scratching herself badly all over her arms as she did so, and fashioned a makeshift bra with the shredded polythene remains. If she ever found out who had stolen her bag and her clothes, she would impale him by the balls on those spikes, she thought. It had to be a 'him', after all. No woman would have left another woman in such a predicament.

Anna began the painful ascent, stubbing her toe on almost every stone she passed. She was halfway to the road, already feeling like she had crawled all the way from Camden to Heraklion when she looked up and saw a figure looming over her – the familiar figure of someone she knew.

'Anna?'

'Vangelis.' Anna wrapped her arms tightly around her top half.

'What happened? You're . . .'

'Someone stole my clothes. My bag, my . . . everything.'

'Hang on,' he said. Looking away to spare Anna's blushes, Vangelis was already stripping off his T-shirt. 'Have this.'

Anna took it gratefully.

'And these.' Vangelis took off his sandals.

'But . . .'

'My feet aren't as delicate as yours. You're getting scratched.'

When Anna was sort of dressed, Vangelis pulled her up the last few feet to the path.

'Did you see anyone?' Anna asked.

Vangelis shook his head. 'No. But you have to be careful where you leave your things. People are desperate.'

'But leaving me with no clothes?'

'I expect whoever it was thought you would be wearing a swimming costume.'

'Well, I wasn't,' Anna sighed.

'We'll go to the police,' said Vangelis. 'But I don't hold out much hope. Was there money in the bag?'

'Yes. But not my passport, thank goodness. And you really didn't see anyone?'

'No.'

'Will you walk back with me to the villa? Only I'm getting a bit cold and you're not exactly dressed for a stroll now you've given me your shirt.'

'Of course. But we won't go that way. This way's quicker.'

Vangelis pointed to the mouth of a cave tunnel that Anna hadn't previously noticed.

Anna licked her lips hesitantly. Dark, confined places had never been her thing, hence her reluctance to join a prestigious tomb hunt in Egypt. And perhaps the thief who had taken her bag was hiding out in there. But Vangelis had already taken her hand. 'It's much easier to go back this way, Anna. Not so much uphill.'

'I don't know . . . I . . .'

'Come on.'

Anna followed him under duress, hoping that it would be just a short trip in the dark anyway, but once they were inside the cave, it quickly became pitch-black and if there was light at the other end of the tunnel, it certainly wasn't within sight. She grasped Vangelis's hand tightly. It was hard enough trying to walk on ground she could actually see in Vangelis's huge sandals. In the darkness of the cave, every step was treacherous.

'This cave doesn't get filled up by the tide, does it?' Anna asked desperately.

'I don't know. But if it does, perhaps in a hundred years someone like us will come and dig us out and put us in their history books.'

'Don't tease me, Vangelis,' Anna protested, though his joke had made her grip his hand tighter still. She might as well have closed her eyes to get a better idea of where they were going. She wondered if her poor night vision was the legacy of a lifelong aversion to carrots. Then suddenly, she felt something brush across the top of her head, making her shriek as though she was trying to scream out her lungs.

'What was that? What was that?' she yelled.

Anna let go of Vangelis's hand and instead flung both her arms right round his body and clung to him like a limpet to a rock. He responded in kind to comfort her until the shrieking stopped. When it did, she still clung to him, staring into the darkness. She was totally unable to see what had touched her just as she was unable to see even Vangelis's face.

'I think it must have been a bat,' Vangelis

reassured her. 'They're OK, they only eat insects, not English girls.'

'Great. That doesn't mean I want it trailing its dirty claws through my hair.'

'It was probably more frightened of you than you are of it.'

'I don't think so.'

'Shall we go on?'

'I can't. I'm sorry. You can stay here but I'm going back the way I came.'

'That would be a waste of time. We're over half-way there now.'

'I'm terrified.'

'Come here.'

But Anna wasn't about to budge. Vangelis pulled her closer for a while. He was prepared to give her just a little more time to calm down. With her head against his bare chest, she could hear his heart beating quickly, she thought. Or was it the sound of her own heart racing, amplified through her ears?

Vangelis knew that his heart was racing but it wasn't because of the bat. He licked his lips nervously and tried to ascertain the position of Anna's mouth in the darkness. He sought out her chin with his hand to help get her face into position. Then, as unexpected as the bat that swept down from the ceiling, Vangelis brushed his lips against hers.

'What are you doing?' she yelped.

'I'm kissing you.'

'Well don't kiss me, just get me out of here.'

Vangelis let Anna go abruptly and stepped away from her. Not far, but far enough.

'Vangelis,' she shrieked desperately, reaching out for him in the pitch-black. 'Vangelis! Where have you gone?'

'I'm right here.'

'I can't see you. Touch me.'

'You just told me not to.'

'I told you not to kiss me. You can hold my hand.'

'No way. I'll see you later.'

The blood pounded in Anna's ears as she heard Vangelis's footsteps heading away from her. She stumbled blindly after him, until she collided with his back and found herself in his arms again, as he struggled to keep them both upright.

'Now you're throwing yourself at me,' he joked.

'Don't try to be funny. Just get me out of here.'

'OK.' He smoothed her hair and returned to holding her hand. 'Look.' He pointed ahead of him and Anna saw the faint shape of his hand in a ghostly glimmer of light. 'There's the other end.'

'Thank God for that,' she sighed, feeling her heart start to slow down again immediately. 'Let's run for it.'

'No. Don't run in here. You might fall over. Besides, I think you should use this opportunity to overcome your fear of the dark. You'll never be able to be a good archaeologist if you don't like caves.'

'I'll stick to open digs, thanks.'

'It would be a shame to confine yourself to such boring things. Digging up Roman fence-posts? Finding the odd Saxon pot? Don't you want to go raiding tombs like Howard Carter?'

'Not really.' Though in fact, it was one of her greatest regrets that her fear had stopped her from investigating the grave of a prince they thought might be even greater than Tutankhamun.

'Come on. Let's just sit here for a while,' Vangelis suggested. 'You can see the other end of the tunnel so you know there's nothing to be scared of.'

In the darkness, Vangelis found himself a ledge and sat down upon it. He pulled Anna over to sit beside him.

'See, nothing to be scared of at all.'

'What is this? Aversion therapy?'

'I suppose. Sometimes we have to confront our fears. I used to be afraid of spiders, you know.'

'You? I can't believe that.'

'It's true. I was terrified of them. If I found one in my bedroom, I had to ask my mother to come and take it away for me. If I was alone in the house, and I saw one hanging from the ceiling, I would find myself paralysed with fear. I couldn't move from the spot I had frozen in until someone came home to rescue me.'

Anna laughed softly.

'Stupid, wasn't I? To let a little thing like a spider stop me from moving about in my own house?'

'How did you cure yourself?'

'I didn't. My big brother decided that he would cure me instead. He took me out to one of the sheep sheds, tied me to a post and dropped spiders on my head until I stopped screaming. It took two days.'

'You're joking.'

'Of course. It took two minutes in reality. But you see, you've been in this cave for five minutes now and for the last minute you haven't even been thinking about where you are. You've been thinking about how silly I was to hate bugs.'

'That's true,' said Anna with a weak laugh. 'You're a genius. And I must be cured. Can we go now?'

'One more minute.'

Anna felt Vangelis's hand on the side of her face again, and before she could protest, he was kissing her once more. For a moment, Anna found herself relaxing into his embrace. Maybe it was the adrenaline. Maybe it was just that his kiss was so nice. Soon Anna found herself wrapping her arms around his neck and going in for his tongue.

He tasted so good: a mixture of the Turkish delight he was always stuffing and the cigarettes Miranda had encouraged him to take up once more. It was a strange combination, but delicious. Anna couldn't get enough of it.

All the pent-up sexual energy which had been bursting out in her dreams since she had arrived in Crete, seemed to gather itself behind Anna's lips now. The barriers were crumbling away like a sand-castle before the breakers on the shore. Vangelis held her so tightly and tenderly. In response, Anna started to let her hands wander over the muscles she had only ever admired from the other side of a dusty site. Then Vangelis slid his hands beneath the borrowed T-shirt and gently caressed Anna's breasts. His thumbs brushed her nipples which quickly puckered in delight.

They said nothing, but soon the cave seemed to be filled with noise. Their breathing, growing faster and more excited, the occasional moan as someone found a particularly delicious spot in which to touch the other. Anna didn't feel cold any more. In fact, she was beginning to sweat. She felt the glow of arousal spreading across her chest and up her slender neck, as if she were trying physiologically to draw Vangelis's attention to the places she wanted – no, needed – to be kissed.

Anna gave a small gasp of surprise as Vangelis touched her clitoris through the soft wet cotton of her knickers.

'Do you want to do it?' he asked her breathlessly.

His words broke the spell. Anna pushed back from him. 'No. No. We can't. I'm . . .' She struggled to find the words.

'Anna,' Vangelis said. 'I think I am falling in love with you.'

That was too much. Now suddenly, the only face

in Anna's mind was Justin's. Smiling, laughing, reminding her of the happy times they had had together. Making her feel guilty.

Anna stood up abruptly, pushing Vangelis away.

'Come on,' she said in a forced bright voice, as she strode as purposefully as she was able towards the light. 'I need some dry clothes. I've got to make a police report.'

She stumbled. 'Wait,' Vangelis said, as he caught up with her and wrapped his arms around her waist again. He began to nuzzle the back of her neck. 'You need to hold on to me.' Anna closed her eyes and tried to bear it. Tried to stop herself from crying.

'Vangelis,' she said slowly. 'Just get me out of this place.'

He let go of her reluctantly, offering his arm for support as they navigated the last part of the tunnel.

When the house was in sight, Anna felt an almost palpable sense of relief.

'I'll go to the police station tomorrow,' she told

him, disappearing into her room before he could protest. Once inside, she collapsed on to the bed, her head on the notepad she had been using to write a letter to Justin, and cried.

Chapter Seventeen

'Look, you stupid little man,' William hissed at the bored-looking police inspector. 'We're not talking about some tourist having his cheapo camera nicked here, I'm talking about the theft of what could turn out to be the most important archaeological find this century.'

The police inspector's junior colleague, who had a slightly better smattering of English, translated everything, including the bit about his boss being stupid and little, with more than a hint of satisfaction.

'We are doing everything we can,' replied the inspector dryly.

'What do you mean?' William exploded. 'You haven't closed the airport. You haven't set up road blocks. You should be checking the luggage of every single person who leaves this country. Making house to house searches. Stopping people in their cars. If I let it slip to the newspapers that the Cretan police stood by and twiddled their thumbs while a common thief made off with a great big chunk of their history, there would be a bloody national scandal. An international scandal. You ought to be informing Interpol, you obnoxious little twit . . .'

'William.' Miranda placed a calming hand on William's arm. 'I think perhaps we ought to go outside and cool down before they throw you in the cells.'

'Don't patronise me, woman,' said William, shaking Miranda's hand away. 'Help me make this greasy bastard understand how important this whole thing is.'

'William, I think we need to talk,' Miranda persisted.

'Not now, for heaven's sake. Why is it that all you bloody women want to do is talk? We've only been sleeping together for a couple of days.'

When that was translated, more than a few eyebrows were raised.

'I'll forget you said that,' hissed Miranda, hiding her blushes. 'But I really must insist that you come outside with me right now. I can't stand by and watch you make an idiot of yourself.' She tightened her grip on his arm and led him towards the door. 'You won't thank me for what I am about to tell you, but ten minutes down the line, you'll be glad that I did.'

'What do you mean?'

'Just follow me.'

She led him outside into the town square and made him sit next to her on a bench beneath an olive tree. Then she took a deep breath and began her story.

'William, there never was a precious vase . . .'

William knitted his brows together in confusion.

'That vase wasn't nearly two millennia old. I had it made last week.'

Miranda could see from William's expression that her words weren't really sinking in.

'It was a fake, William. A remarkably realistic copy, but a fake. I had it made by a bloke in the village, then I chipped a bit off and rubbed dirt all over it. I didn't really think you'd fall for it,' she added, as an afterthought.

'But . . . but—' William stuttered.

'But I put it in the right place, I guess. And that must have been what confused you. I was going to let you in on the joke that evening at the site, when we first made love. But you seemed so happy.'

'I was ecstatic.'

'I didn't want to upset you.'

'So now you've ruined my life?'

'Don't say that.'

'But it's true. You have ruined it. Why? Why would you do such a terrible thing?'

'Because,' said Miranda slowly. 'You ruined my life first.'

'What do you mean?'

'Don't pretend you don't know, William. This is about me and Adam Buchanan. You threatened him, didn't you? You told him that if he didn't stop seeing me you'd tell the whole thing to his wife.'

'Oh, God.' William suddenly slumped forward, head in his hands. 'You did this because of him? He told you that I threatened him? Told him to tell you that the affair had run its course?'

'Well, it hadn't. We were madly in love with each other,' said Miranda dramatically.

'Oh, God,' William muttered again.

'You told him to stop seeing me because you hated me.'

'Oh, Miranda,' William sighed. 'Nothing could be further from the truth. I told him to stop seeing you because I couldn't bear the thought of you being hurt. Adam has always had affairs, for as long as I've known him. And often more than one at a time. Just two weeks after we got back from that dig in

Cyprus he started to see another girl, as well as you. She was a first-year undergraduate. Barely eighteen years old. I couldn't stand the thought of you falling more and more deeply for his lies.'

'It's not true,' Miranda protested. 'He was only seeing me. He told me so.'

'And what do you think he tells his wife, for heaven's sake? Deception is a habit for Adam. A hobby. Lying to three women is not that much harder than lying to two. Miranda, I lost my own wife to Adam Buchanan's treacherous charms.'

Just then a police officer came out to inform them that the inspector was ready to take a statement. William waved him away. 'It doesn't matter now,' he said sadly. The policeman looked confused. 'You can stop the search. There's been a terrible mistake.'

'I've been an idiot, haven't I?' said Miranda.

'Love makes fools of us all. But, what I really don't understand is why you slept with me if you hated me so much?'

'I guess I just discovered that I didn't hate you after all.'

'The sex was rather good, wasn't it?' William ventured carefully.

Miranda nodded and reached out to take his hand. The sex,' she assured him, 'was mind-blowing.'

William's glum expression was quickly flooded out by a grin. 'That's good to hear,' he told her. 'Don't suppose you fancy going up to the site for a quick poke about right now? To look for artefacts, I mean . . .'

Chapter Eighteen

It must be over between me and Justin now, Anna told herself. She had been unfaithful again. How easy it had been to slip into Vangelis's willing arms. And if Anna had let that happen, even though she claimed to feel so much for Justin, then she could almost be certain that Justin had been doing the same to her with any number of girls he met in the City bars after work. The thought of him touching another woman made her start to feel sick.

She could hear sounds floating towards her room from the kitchen. Dinner was being prepared. She had just half an hour before she had to face Vangelis again.

Anna got to her feet and stumbled across to the bathroom. She turned the taps on full and ran a deep, deep bath. The smell of Vangelis's sun-warmed skin was still on her hands, taunting her with memories. Though not all of them were bad.

'What's wrong with you tonight?' Miranda asked as they shared a post-dinner cigarette on the front steps. 'You hardly looked at Vangelis all evening. You two haven't had another fight, I hope?'

'No,' said Anna, stubbing out what remained of the cigarette on the bottom of her sandal. 'We haven't had a fight. In fact, we did quite the opposite.'

'Quite the opposite?'

'I went for a swim. Some bastard stole my clothes while I was in the water. Vangelis rescued me, I suppose. We walked back here through a tunnel and it just happened.'

'You mean you had sex with Vangelis?' asked Miranda excitedly.

'We just kissed . . .' said Anna.

'Oh, boring. But what was it like?'

'Wonderful. Tender. Better than any kisses I've had in the past three years.'

'Then what's your problem?'

Anna shrugged. 'You know.'

'The boy back home?'

Anna nodded.

Miranda took hold of her friend's face and turned it towards her own, as if she were about to address a naughty child.

'Look, forget him. He hasn't written. He hasn't called. He hasn't flown out here and turned up on the doorstep begging forgiveness. He's not worthy of your concern. And you've already been unfaithful twice,' she reminded her with a wicked smile. 'Have a holiday fling if you feel like it. You deserve one.'

'But I don't want a fling,' Anna protested. 'And I've got an awful feeling that neither does Vangelis. I don't want to hurt him.'

Miranda gave a little snort of amusement.

'You won't hurt him. If he's been giving you all the usual love flannel, then all I can say is you should know better. Most men talk in the language of love when they want sex. And for women it's vice versa,' she added as she got to her feet. 'Listen, I've got to go. I promised William I'd meet him up at the dig. You know, he's a lot better at the sex thing than I expected, but he always wants to do it among the artefacts and it isn't exactly comfortable.'

'Perhaps you can teach him to do it in a proper bed when you get back to England. Unless you're planning to leave him behind, like all your other broken hearts.'

'Darling,' said Miranda. 'For the first time ever, I think I might try and continue a relationship past the customs desk. I think things are changing for me. I spent the afternoon telling the truth, believe it or not. And when he found out about the vase, William still wanted to know me. I think he really, really likes me. Cares for me, even. I could do with some of that.'

Anna nodded in tacit agreement.

'Better not keep him waiting then.'

Up at the site, William was already waiting for Miranda to arrive. When he saw her coming, he instinctively got to his feet.

'No need to stand for me,' she told him, waving him to sit back down on the wall. She sat down beside him. In his hands he had a piece of pottery, with the edge of some kind of painting on it.

'What's that?' Miranda asked.

'I'm not sure. I found it just a moment ago, while I was waiting for you. It looks a bit like the one we lost, don't you think?'

Miranda took the shard from William's hand and turned it over between her own. It did indeed look a bit like a piece from the vase that Nicky's brother had faked for her.

'I don't want to get too excited,' William continued. 'I mean, perhaps this one is a fake as well. But if we were to find a genuine vase similar to the rutting Minotaur one, then the future of this site would be settled. I was wondering, if you don't mind, if we might keep our hands off each other for a short while and have a bit of a dig about.'

Miranda was about to protest, but seeing William look so excited, she couldn't help but relent.

They shone a strong light on to the ground at their feet and began to work. It seemed as though William was right. There was another vase there. And this was one that Miranda didn't know anything about. Soon they had enough little shards to piece together the base of the new find and start to see what kind of picture might have been painted on to the side. Miranda's jaw dropped open in surprise when she saw the scene that was taking shape. A man and a woman. She: naked to the waist. He: lifting her skirts and entering her in more or less the same way as the minotaur on the fake vase had been ravishing the queen.

'I don't believe it,' she murmured.

'You look even more shocked by this vase than you were when I found the minotaur piece,' said William with a sly smile. 'Shame it's not anywhere near as well preserved.'

'No, but . . .' Miranda stuttered. 'This is more shocking because I'm pretty sure that it's real.'

'Well, let's not tell the others what we've found until we're sure. I don't want to raise anybody's hopes unnecessarily.'

'Good idea.'

'Does it make you feel as sexy as the other vase?' William asked suddenly.

'More,' said Miranda quietly. And it really did. This, after all, was a real piece of history that she held in her hands.

'Want to do something about it?' said William as he unzipped his fly and Miranda fell happily to her knees on the dirt.

'Mmm.' A sigh like escaping steam flowed from William's mouth. The moment Miranda's lips closed oh-so-gently on his purple penis, he took her blonde head in his hands. As her tongue worked diligently around the tip, he scrunched up great handfuls of her hair, even rubbing some of it against his own downy stomach. Miranda wasn't a deep throater. She liked to use her hands and her tongue, gently massaging the foreskin up and down the shaft with her fingers while her tongue flickered across the smooth glans and sensitive raphe. She closed her eyes and savoured the taste of his clean penis, growing saltier with semen as she licked him, and listened eagerly for the sighs that let her know she was doing it right. She worked all over the shaft with her tongue and right down to his balls. William's hands were going mad in her hair, twisting and pulling harder than he knew, but Miranda bore his clumsiness for now, guessing that it was a sign of deep, deep appreciation.

Letting his glans drag slowly out over her full bottom lip, Miranda moved her attention to his balls. She blew gently on the hairy sacs which hung swollen and pulsing between his hard thighs. William's pelvis bucked forward in appreciation. Next Miranda cupped one ball in each hand and fondled them delicately while she licked sporadically at the bobbing glans before her. William was getting really hot now and Miranda had to use one hand to hold the shaft still while she licked at it.

'Miranda . . .' He breathed her name as though it were a word he had only just learned. His fingers tightened in her hair. 'Slow down, slow down, please,' he begged her. 'I feel like I'm going to burst with excitement and I only want to come inside you.'

Reluctantly unfastening her tingling hands from his shaft first, William pulled Miranda up from her knees so that they were face to face once more. When he kissed her again, her mouth was salty with his own semen.

'You want to come inside me?' Miranda asked coquettishly. 'You'll have to get me turned on first.'

He shuddered with delight at the prospect. Still kissing her, he slid his hand beneath her shirt and made straight for her nipples. But that wasn't going to be enough for Miranda. Not tonight.

'Do you know Latin?' she asked him cheekily.

William raised his head from where he was kissing her nipples into hardness and said testily, 'Of course I do.'

'Then you'll be familiar with the term "cunnilingus".' She smiled.

This time it was William's turn to get on his knees.

Miranda parted her legs and stood above William like a dominatrix. She placed one hand on his head to guide him in the right direction and hitched up her dust-covered skirt with the other. William took off his glasses and moved forward, tongue stretched. He used his hands to part her labia as he sought out her most secret place. Miranda looked up at the stars and quivered with anticipation. She knew she was wet already. Holding William's magnificent hard-on in her hot little hands had already seen to that.

Down below, she felt William's tongue make that first delicious contact with her clitoris. She shivered delightedly, and shifted her position so that he could better reach her. In her mind, she tried to visualise the scene as if watched by a voyeur. She reached for the buttons of her shirt and started to undo them one by one to reveal the perfect breasts that William had warmed with his kisses. She would want anyone watching to have a fantastic view. As William worked himself into a frenzy between her thighs, Miranda slid her hand round a firm, full breast and began to stroke at her nipple. It was already as hard and sensitive as her swollen clitoris.

'Keep going,' Miranda commanded when it seemed as though William was flagging. 'Keep going.' She tugged at his hair to warn him what might happen if he stopped. She luxuriated in the feeling of her breasts swinging freely in the night air.

'That's right,' Miranda breathed like a serpent. She pulled gently on William's hair again to encourage him to work faster still.

William closed his eyes and breathed in the aroma of her beautiful pussy. Each breath he took filled his lungs with the scent of her, a scent almost as arousing as the sight of her fantastic body.

Up above him, Miranda moaned contentedly and bucked her hips forward again. Encouraged that he was doing well, William decided to change his tactics. From long strokes with his tongue, he moved to take Miranda's clitoris gently between his teeth. At this, Miranda gasped, but she didn't push him away. The unexpected sensation on the edge of pain was enough to give her the first faint shiver of an orgasm. But then it subsided again. William hadn't finished.

'Lick me again,' she begged him. 'Lick me and finger me at the same time.' William obliged, thrusting his finger inside her as he licked at her clitoris. Miranda gasped, and laughed and shuddered. She wanted to fall to the floor and writhe on the earth, but William held her upright and kept on licking, his strokes growing more confident and harder until Miranda had to stuff her hand into her mouth to stop her from screaming as she started to come.

Back and forth Miranda's hips bucked, pushing her pussy into William's face again and again, until he got to his feet and started to kiss her. At the same time, he wrapped his hand around his rock-hard penis and slicked his foreskin back and forward frantically. He didn't want to miss the moment, and he didn't. Before Miranda finished coming, William was coming too. Great hot jets of semen burst from his penis and splattered against Miranda's naked thighs. The sensation of the sticky, sweet cum landing on her skin sent Miranda into further spasms, until they both collapsed on to the ground, laughing and coming and kissing.

When it seemed as though an eternity had passed with them just lying there watching the stars move across the sky, Miranda got unsteadily to her feet. As she pushed herself upright, her hand felt the sharp edge of a piece of pottery. Picking it up and holding it to the faint light of William's guttering lamp, she saw that she had found another piece of the pot. She didn't know much about Minoan script, but she thought that the word written upon it might be 'love'.

Chapter Nineteen

Anna was almost asleep when she heard the knock at her door. Thinking it was part of a dream, she ignored it the first time. Next time, the person who was knocking called out to her too.

'Anna? Are you in there?' For once, her midnight visitor wasn't Miranda. It was Vangelis.

Anna sat up in bed and wrapped the sheet around her naked body defensively. What did he want? Well, she knew what he wanted. But why didn't he see that he couldn't have it? Anna didn't answer him. Instead, now fully awake, she just stared at the firmly closed door, hoping that she would soon hear his footsteps beating a retreat.

But he wasn't about to give up.

'Anna. I want to talk to you.'

Anna bit her lip, keeping her silence.

Suddenly her bedroom door creaked open.

'I'm sorry,' said Vangelis. 'But I knew you would be in here. I just heard you finish typing. I thought that you wouldn't be asleep yet.'

'Well I was,' said Anna, pulling the sheet ever tighter around her. 'What do you want?'

'I want to know what I have done to upset you. You wouldn't even look at me at dinner this evening. I thought that after what happened in the cave . . .'

'Well, you thought wrong,' Anna snapped. 'What happened in the cave was a mistake.'

'I don't think so.'

Vangelis was still standing in the doorway, silhouetted by the light from his own room. 'Can I come in?' he asked.

'I want to get some sleep,' Anna protested.

'For a moment, that's all. I just want to talk to you for a moment, so that we can go back to being normal. If we have to.'

It was a persuasive argument. Anna still had to share a house with him for another couple of weeks and she didn't want it to be an uncomfortable experience. Perhaps he would listen to what she had to say about Justin and accept that she and Vangelis couldn't be more than friends.

Vangelis crossed the room slowly and sat down on the end of her bed. There really was nowhere else to sit. The chair by the dressing table was covered in piles of clothes. Underwear. Things that Vangelis probably thought almost as out of bounds as Anna herself.

'Anna . . .'

'Vangelis . . .'

They both tried to begin their arguments at once.

'You go first,' Anna conceded.

'No, you.'

'OK. If you insist. Vangelis, I have to put this bluntly. What we did this afternoon was a mistake.

I have a boyfriend back in England. You know that. He hasn't been in touch much since I came out here to Crete but equally things haven't been resolved between us yet and until they are, I can't be with anyone else. It's not that I wouldn't want to . . . but I can't. Do you understand?'

Even in the semi-darkness of the room, she could tell that Vangelis was gazing straight at her.

'No,' he began. 'No, I don't understand. If he hasn't contacted you since you arrived here, then it must be over.'

Anna shook her head in protest.

'It is over and you should forget him. We have fun together. We like each other a lot. What's wrong with that?'

'Nothing's wrong with that. For some people. But I need more.'

'I can give you more.'

'No, don't even say it.'

But Anna let Vangelis slide his arm around her shoulders as she put a finger to his lips.

'I wouldn't say anything I didn't mean.'

He tried to kiss her then, first planting a little dry peck on her cheek. Anna twisted to escape him, but he was insistent. She needed to be persuaded, he knew. Vangelis reached out for her face again and cupped her chin in his hand, then, ever so gently, he pulled her lips towards his and covered them with the softest kiss imaginable.

'No,' she protested quietly. 'I don't want to do this.'

'You say that every time,' he said a little angrily. 'Perhaps I shouldn't keep trying to persuade you. But I can't help thinking that you'd really quite like to say yes.'

She smiled at his audacity, but still moved away from him slightly and unconsciously let her hair fall over her face like a mask to hide her shyness. But Vangelis wouldn't give up. He reached out and pushed the curtain of hair away so that he could see her eyes again. She turned her head away from him playfully.

'Vangelis, please don't encourage me.'

'I don't want you to do anything against your will,' he said softly, shuffling along the bed to be closer to her. 'That isn't the point at all.' He took her chin in his hand once more and stole another kiss. And another. And another. Until Anna could no longer bring herself to resist. She did want him. She wanted him every time she saw him. And what harm could it really do if she gave in to him now? She had already almost given in to him once, down on the beach. The chains of her fidelity had already been broken.

With this in mind, Anna kissed him back hungrily. As much as she tried to deny it to herself and to him, there was something about Vangelis that she couldn't resist. When he wrapped his arms around her, it was as though something clicked into place inside.

Now that Vangelis's lips moved away from her face and down the slope of her long neck, Anna was able to murmur, 'Yes'.

She loved the softness of his touch. The sinewy lines of his snake-like body. His hips, almost as narrow as her own. His hard but warm buttocks. The comforting smell of his skin, which would for ever after remind her of the sun beating down on the sand on a red-hot day.

Soon, she found herself lying beneath him on the bed, allowing him to kiss a hot trail up her quivering stomach towards her breasts. She closed her eyes and ran her hands over his shoulders. In spite of herself, she knew that she was growing more and more aroused, almost unbearably so. All her good intentions were lining up at the open window and throwing themselves out.

Why shouldn't she have what she wanted? something deep inside asked. Vangelis slid his hand past the elastic of her knickers and this time she didn't protest. Her own hands had moved from his shoulders to his buttocks. She kissed him roughly, jabbing her tongue into his mouth and almost before she knew it, she felt his penis echoing her tongue between her legs.

They moved like two parts of the same machine. It was as though they had been lovers for ever as their bodies moved together and apart, together and apart, increasing the arousal between them with each stroke. Anna covered Vangelis's neck with kisses as he pushed her closer to ecstasy. In return, Vangelis bit her neck and dug his fingers deep into her buttocks. Anna drew breath sharply at the exquisite pain.

Then, for whatever reason, the tension of the moment suddenly being released perhaps, Anna suddenly had the urge to laugh out loud. She exploded with laughter just as Vangelis reached his climax. He came shudderingly, his face confused by her expression. Then he collapsed on top of her and before long, he was laughing too.

'I don't know what came over me just then,' she said, almost apologising when he had rolled off to lay beside her. 'Except that I wasn't laughing because you were funny, you understand. It was because you were fabulous. I've never felt so relaxed in my whole life.'

And it was true. It was as though making love to Vangelis had shaken every last bit of stress and tension from her body. She felt calm, complete, cleansed. As though she had let herself be led out of the darkness of her unhappiness to a better place.

People often talked about sexual healing, Anna thought, but this was the first time she had believed that it was anything other than a cheesy metaphor.

As they lay side by side, still as two statues on a tomb, doing nothing but feeling the soft sea-breeze caress their bodies, Anna thought she might have accidentally stumbled upon perfection. Then, closing her eyes, she began to drift into sleep. Within minutes, she began to dream. First Miranda's face loomed above her from out of the darkness. Then Justin's. He didn't look happy at all.

'I thought we had something special,' he told her accusingly. 'I thought we were going to be together for ever and ever. But this is how you betray me. With someone who only wants you for your body.'

'Only wants your body,' repeated the dream-monster Miranda. 'I say, go for it, girl.'

'Go for it if you like, Anna. But we're over,' said Justin. 'We're over, over, over . . .'

'No,' Anna called feebly. 'No! I just need to know how you feel. I just need you to say that you love me.'

She awoke to Vangelis's concerned smile, but the dream was still so vivid in her head that she half expected to see Justin standing behind him.

'Go,' she said, suddenly pushing Vangelis out of the bed. 'Please go. I need to be alone.'

He tried to steal one last kiss. She let him have it grudgingly, then physically pushed him from her bed. When the door closed again behind him, Anna collapsed on to the pillows and started to cry big wet tears of confusion.

Chapter Twenty

This is ridiculous, thought Anna, as the next morning at breakfast, she found herself trying to pretend that nothing had happened between her and Vangelis. He, for his part, was at least being decent enough to lay off the meaningful stares over toast. In fact, he looked quite nonchalant. Perhaps he was feeling that way too, Anna began to think. Perhaps he had had what he wanted and now he would happily go back to being just her friend. The thought caught in her throat and made her feel like she was about to cry again.

'Something wrong?' William asked her. Miranda and Vangelis turned to see what had attracted William's attention.

'Just a bit of toast,' she said. 'Went down the wrong way.'

'Have some juice,' said Vangelis, pushing his half-full glass across the table. Their fingers brushed lightly as Anna reached for the juice, but she didn't look up to see his smile.

'It's my birthday today,' William announced suddenly.

'Oh, Willy,' Miranda sighed. 'Why didn't you tell me?'

'Didn't want to make a fuss. It's terrible if you make a fuss and everyone still forgets.'

'I wouldn't have forgotten,' Miranda protested. 'We've got to have some kind of celebration. I saw a cake shop in the village. No, I've got a better idea, let's go to the taverna and get pissed.'

'The taverna?' said Anna incredulously. They hadn't been to the taverna since Miranda decided that she would dump Nicky the Greek for her boss.

'Are you sure that's a good idea? You know how William is on the raki,' she added, as if that were the only reason.

'I insist. Besides, it's Cretan night tonight. First of the summer season. There'll be traditional dancing.'

'Ohmigod,' said Anna.

'And local wine.'

'They use the same stuff to run the mopeds out here,' said Vangelis.

'You wouldn't have a better time at Stringfellows,' added Miranda.

'I wouldn't go to Stringfellows,' said Anna flatly.

'Sometimes,' said Miranda, 'you are such a spoilsport.'

And Vangelis looked at Anna as though he agreed.

So the date was set. As soon as it was too dark to dig any longer, the happy archaeologists trooped back to the house to get ready for William's big birthday bash. Miranda had been trying to winkle his age out of him all day long, but only got as far as discovering that he was old enough to have seen The Clash play live, and not on their retirement tour.

An hour after getting back to the house, most of which time was allocated to helping Miranda do up the thousand buttons on the back of her new sundress, they were ready to go. William and Miranda stepped off down the path to the village first, arm in arm. Anna and Vangelis brought up the rear, keeping a polite distance between the people in front of them and between themselves. The conversation never strayed from the subject of national dances.

Once inside the taverna, Vangelis quickly disappeared to the bar to get drinks, while Miranda and Anna hunted for the table with the best view. William was sent to hunt out tobacco.

'Still getting your share of Greek godliness?' Miranda asked subtly.

Anna shook her head. 'I shouldn't have done it. Let's not talk about it, eh?'

Vangelis brought them their drinks, but he didn't sit down with them. He explained that he had seen an old friend, the sister of a man with whom he had studied in Athens. He jerked his head in the direction of the bar to indicate the girl he was talking about and she waved shyly back. Her name was Clio, Vangelis explained, and her family owned most of the village.

'If she's rich,' meowed Miranda, 'then how come she gets to be so beautiful as well? Fat ankles, though.'

Anna tried to remain uninterested as she watched Vangelis rejoin Clio at the bar. Now that he was standing next to her, the Greek girl's shy veneer had been replaced by a confident grin, and she gave a casual hair toss that suggested that she knew she had everything to be happy about. She looked like a young Sophia Loren, with thick black hair that tumbled down her bare back in her strappy sundress like a well-loved horse's mane.

Anna stopped watching Clio when Vangelis said something that made her laugh and she ran her elegant fingers down his thick, well-muscled forearm.

'Dancing started yet?'

It was William, returned from his mission to find Miranda the only packet of Marlboro Lights left on the whole island.

'They wouldn't start the dancing without the birthday boy,' purred Miranda. 'Thank you for these, my darling.'

He leaned forward for a kiss of gratitude, but got an eye full of smoke ring instead.

The musicians had set up their instruments and on the dance floor, five surprisingly young children lined up to start the first dance. They looked terribly serious as they made their way through the traditional steps, accepted the applause politely, then they bravely took up the challenge of showing the tourists how it was done.

Miranda dragged William on to the floor to do an impression of Zorba the Greek in a dance that seemed to end up pretty much like a conga. Once or twice, the master of ceremonies swept around the room, trying to encourage the wallflowers to join in. Anna waved him away firmly and was left alone. Over at the bar, still talking to Clio, Vangelis, too, resisted all attempts to bring him into the fray.

But soon the traditional dances were over. The child dancers went home to get some sleep – school term had yet to finish. The musicians packed away their instruments and the sound of bouzouki was replaced by a crackly taped mix of classic 1980s smooches. Anna smiled wistfully when George Michael began to sing 'Careless Whisper'. She could look back on that song with fondness, because it reminded her not of Justin, but of Ryan Law, whose life's mission had been to undo her bra with one hand when he should have been revising for his A-levels.

'You dancing?' Miranda asked William, as she dragged him to his feet again. He protested weakly, but soon the incongruous couple were shuffling around the floor.

Anna felt suddenly very alone. She hadn't wanted to join in with the Greek dancing, but now . . . Over by the bar she could see Phil the fisherman, whom she had so successfully managed to avoid since that night on the boat, suddenly catch sight of her. He raised his eyebrows in invitation. Anna looked deep into her glass and hoped that he would take the hint. When she looked up again however, he was walking towards her. But so was Vangelis. Thank God, she thought. Vangelis would rescue her. But instead he walked straight on past her and into the waiting arms of Clio, leaving Anna stranded and helpless in the cross-eyed sights of Phil.

'Pretty lady, are you all on your own?' he asked.

Anna shrugged. 'I'm happy just sitting here watching the dancing, thank you very much. Alone,' she added, but he wasn't about to be put off.

'Let me dance with you. My name is Phil. What is your name?'

God, he didn't even remember her! Vangelis had been right. There had probably been a dozen English girls in the taverna since that night on the boat, and Phil had tried his cheesy lines with every single one of them. Now he was grinning inanely at her, totally unaware that she already knew his game very well indeed.

'Let me put my arms around you and make you smile once more.'

She could think of nothing worse. Anna suddenly got to her feet and pushed Phil rudely out of the way as she made a dash for the garden. But once outside, all she could think of was the sight of Vangelis and Clio whirling around the dance floor as though they were destined to be together. Their two bodies moved like one body, joined together in perfect timing. Why did she feel jealous? Why? Why? *Why?*

'Yoo-hoo, Anna! Where are you? We're going back to the villa now.'

Anna stayed silent as she listened to William and Miranda stumbling out into the garden.

'Ah, she'll be all right,' Miranda said. 'I expect she's copped off with some Greek bloke and gone back to his place.'

'Would Anna really do that?' William asked. Anna could hear the shock in his voice.

'If he remembered to say please first,' Miranda laughed. 'She likes her men sophisticated and polite. No bit of rough for her.'

Anna bit hard on her knuckle. To come out of the bushes now would let Miranda know that she had heard everything and Anna just couldn't face the embarrassment of that.

'Let's just leave her,' Miranda persisted. 'She'll find her own way back to the house.'

'I'm not happy about leaving her out here on her own.' Suddenly Vangelis was speaking. 'I'll look for her. You'll walk Clio home, won't you?'

'Oh,' Miranda moaned. 'But she lives so far away from us, and my feet are killing me in these stupid shoes.'

'I'll see you back at the house. Goodnight, Clio.'

Anna could just make out the sound of a dry kiss goodnight. 'Give my regards to your fiancé.'

Anna could have laughed out loud.

'Well, I think you're stupid,' Miranda moaned as her voice faded into the distance. 'You'll only be upset when you discover that she's out on the love boat with fishy Phil. Ha ha ha . . .'

Then Miranda was thankfully too far away to be heard any more. Anna waited in her hiding place still. What else could she do? Suddenly appear to Vangelis and let him know that she had been there all along? No, she waited until she saw him set off down the path, then slipped out of the shadows to follow him . . .

'Vangelis.'

He was almost at the beach before she caught up with him. She laid a hand on his arm and he turned to face her.

'Vangelis, where are you going?'

'I was looking for you,' he told her. His face was stern. 'You ran away from us. Was something wrong?'

Anna shrugged. 'No, nothing was wrong. I just felt like getting some fresh air, that's all.'

'You should have said where you were going first.'

'Why? Are you guys *in loco parentis* or something? I'm a big girl now. Besides, I didn't want to disturb you while you were dancing with your girlfriend.'

'My girlfriend?'

'Yes. Clio. Looks like the two of you are pretty close.'

Vangelis snorted. 'You have a problem with that?'

'Of course not. I was just making an observation.'

'Well, for your information, Clio is engaged to be married to one of my best friends. I have known her since we were both children. She's a friend too, that's all.'

He picked up a stone from the path and hurled it out into the darkness in the vague direction of the sea. 'Though why should I be bothered what you think is going on?'

'You shouldn't be. I mean, it's none of my business. I'm sorry I even mentioned it.'

'I don't know how to handle you, Anna. Last night you pushed me out of bed like you were getting rid of Phil from the taverna. Then tonight, you acted like a spoilt child because I danced with an old friend. What is wrong with you? What do you want?'

Anna opened her mouth to protest but nothing came out.

'Well, at least I know you're safe now,' Vangelis continued. 'I'll see you back at the house in the morning.' Then he set off again on the path down to the sea without looking back to see whether Anna was following. She didn't follow him. Instead she watched his shadow merge with the shadows of the trees, desperately racking her brains for the right thing to say. But she couldn't find it in time.

Chapter Twenty-One

Next morning, Anna was woken early.

'Anna, there is someone here for you.'

Anna got up from bed slowly, expecting it to be that comical Greek policeman again, with more questions that would lead him no further whatsoever to the last resting place of the fake vase (which was in fact at the bottom of the village well). No sooner had William asked them to drop the case, than the police seemed to have thrown themselves behind it with a vengeance. Anna smoothed her hair away from her face and slipped on a cardigan over her nightshirt for decency's sake.

When she reached the bottom of the stairs, Vangelis was there, looking up towards her with big, sorrowful eyes.

'He is in the kitchen,' Vangelis explained. 'I am sure you will want to be alone.'

Her heart beating hesitantly, Anna laid her hand on the door handle. 'Thanks, Vangelis,' she whispered. His reaction had told her who this mystery visitor was likely to be without the need for words.

She opened the kitchen door and stood in the doorway for a while, just looking at the back of his neck. Justin sat at the kitchen table, playing with the remains of his nervously shredded boarding pass. He didn't notice her for a moment, but when he did, he leapt to his feet immediately, ran to her, then hovered inches from holding her as though he hardly knew who she was.

'Surprise!'

'What are you doing here?' she asked accusingly.

'I got your letter. It came on Friday morning. I got a plane ticket out here as soon as I could.'

'My letter?'

'Yes, the dirty one, you minx.'

Anna's mouth gaped open with surprise. It had taken almost a month to reach him.

'I've missed you,' he said. And she knew that he thought he meant it.

'You avoided my calls. You didn't even text.'

'I didn't know what to say to you. You turned down my marriage proposal. Remember?'

'It was hardly a marriage proposal,' Anna corrected. 'You didn't want me to marry you, Justin. You just didn't want me to come out here. You'd have said anything.'

'I'm sorry. I suppose I just needed you to prove how much you felt for me. When I got your letter, I knew.' He hugged her tightly.

Anna just looked at the floor.

'Well? Aren't you glad I'm here?' he asked her.

Anna plastered on a smile. 'Of course I am. It's

just that this is a bit of a surprise. You might have called first.'

'I thought you liked surprises.'

'Yes, I do . . . it's just that . . .' Just that what? Anna asked herself. Just that she had spent all night thinking of ways to patch things up with Vangelis? That her feelings for her Cretan lover had finally kept Justin out of her mind for a whole twenty-four hours?

There was no way they could talk properly in the house, with everyone drifting in and out to fetch food or forgotten bits of paper. Anna told Justin to change into some comfortable shoes. They were going for a walk.

As they set off down the path, Anna couldn't help looking back towards the villa. She was sure she saw a shadow at the window of Vangelis's room but she put it out of her mind. Justin deserved her full attention while she heard him out at least.

Anna didn't know where to go except towards the beach. Pretty soon, Justin was complaining that he had grit in his Birkenstocks. It was the first time his smart new sandals had seen off-road conditions since they left the shop. Anna tried to ignore his bleating as she found the place where the path divided into two and one branch led down towards the sand. She couldn't help thinking of the first time she had stood on that high point, looking down on to the blue sea and wishing that Justin could be there to share the view with her. Now that he was there, he wasn't even looking in the right direction. Instead he was undoing one of his sandals and trying to bang the grit out of it.

'Bloody sandals. I knew I should have worn my trainers,' he muttered.

'Beautiful here, isn't it?' Anna murmured. Justin looked up from his shoes momentarily.

'What? Oh, yes. It's beautiful. Do we have to go down that path to get to the beach?'

'I'm afraid so. The Ministry of Tarmac hasn't got this far yet.'

They picked their way down the cliff, Justin complaining that at any moment he might fall and twist his ankle, never daring to look towards the glittering waves for fear that brief second of bliss would be the second when he also found a loose rock. Anna jumped down the final three feet then held out her arms to catch Justin when he did the same. She didn't remember him being like this. She was sure that on their university field trips he'd been as tough as the best of them. Wearing Gucci loafers in an office all day had obviously softened him up.

'Where now?' he asked when they were finally on the sand.

'Well. We're here, of course. I thought we might sit here on the beach and talk for a while. You could even have a swim. The water's pretty warm. Like a bath when the sun shines.'

'I haven't brought my trunks.'

'You don't need your trunks here. It's hardly Brighton, is it? No one ever comes past, I promise.' She sat down on the sand and almost smiled when she remembered the time that she had been caught out. She unbuckled her sandals and let the hot sand between her toes.

'So this is where you come skinny-dipping, is it?

You and that Greek bloke.' Justin said it without a hint of humour. Anna turned to catch his expression. 'Vangelis. Isn't that his name? Sounds more like a rock group. He seemed a bit disappointed to see me.'

'What do you mean?'

'I mean, he seemed to think that I was an intruder.'

'I'm sure you're getting him wrong,' Anna blustered. 'It's the language barrier. It can make it seem as though he's being a bit short with you sometimes. But he isn't. I promise you.'

'Well, he shouldn't have any reason to be short with me, should he?'

Anna picked up a handful of sand and trickled it over her feet. 'I don't want to talk about him right now. I want to talk about you and me.'

'What is there to discuss? I've said that I'm sorry for not calling you and the minute I got your letter I got on a flight. I thought it would be romantic to surprise you for once. You have no idea of the hell I'm going to catch when I go back into the office. This is a PLS week you know.'

'Of course. A PLS week.' She wasn't sure what the acronym stood for exactly but a PLS week always meant late nights at the office.

'It's not going to do my promotion prospects much good coming out here when there's so much to be done back in London . . . But I decided,' he continued triumphantly, 'that you were more important to me than work. You are the most important thing in my life.'

'Am I?'

'I wouldn't have come out here if you weren't.'

'Why didn't you think that until you got my letter?' she asked a little sadly.

'I was wrapped up in my work. You know that sometimes I just need a little prod to remind me about my priorities.' He smiled nervously and gave her a little prod in the arm to illustrate his point. Anna responded by pretending that his gentle poke had knocked her over into the sand.

'Oh, Justin,' she sighed when she had recovered herself. 'What are we going to do now?'

'I know.'

Justin leaned across their discarded sandals and planted a kiss on Anna's mouth. She couldn't help but respond. The desire she felt for him had been a part of her life for so long that to kiss him back was almost a subconscious reflex. Within seconds he had pushed the sandals out of the way and enveloped her in his arms while he covered her face and neck with kisses as though she were a plump ripe peach and he hadn't eaten for three weeks.

Anna was surprised when she, too, discovered that she had been missing something. His kiss reawakened a memory and suddenly she noticed the void that had grown in her since they had been apart.

After that, it was almost automatic. The same moves, the same sighs, the same sensations that had thrilled Anna for so long followed in rapid succession. Justin unbuttoned her shirt and pushed it from her shoulders. She sighed with pleasure as he kissed first one breast and then the other. Her hand moved straight to the front of his trousers. She could feel his hard-on, warm through the front of his thin cotton chinos. His hand was warm too as it cupped her round breast.

'I have missed you so much,' he kept murmuring, over and over, as if saying it so many times now would make up for the long lonely nights when Anna felt as though she would die from sorrow at Justin's indifference. She tipped back her head and let him kiss her long throat. She let her hands roam over his face and neck too, reminding herself of his beauty through touch.

'Will you come home with me?' he asked her afterwards.

Anna looked into those familiar, magical eyes and was lost. She nodded blindly. Of course she would go back with him. What else could she do? She had to go back to London sometime. Back to the real world. And Justin was the centre of her real world. Their making love on the beach had confirmed that.

'Is that a yes?'

'Yes,' she croaked.

Justin smiled broadly, then kissed her as though she were a five-year-old, giving the correct answer to a question at school.

'Come on,' he said, jumping up and grabbing Anna's hand. 'Let's go back to the villa and start packing up your things right now. There's plenty of space on the flight back to Gatwick this afternoon.'

'This afternoon?' Anna was more shocked than she had been when Justin first arrived. 'You mean, you weren't even planning to stay here overnight?'

'Well,' Justin said patiently. 'I was pretty certain I'd be able to persuade you to come home so I got myself an open return. This way, I can minimise the number of days I have to miss at work. If you hadn't said yes, I would have stayed here until I did persuade you,' he added with a cheeky smile. 'So this afternoon it is.'

'OK.' Anna nodded. 'I suppose.' She got unsteadily to her feet and started to follow him. Far from complaining, this time, Justin breached the tangled path like the mountain goats that lived on Kri-Kri Island. It was Anna who stumbled behind.

By the time they had got back to the empty villa, she wasn't so sure that she had made the right decision. She packed hurriedly, throwing her things into her suitcase. She was contracted to do another week on the dig, but Justin assured her that he would make up for the money she lost by not working out the full week. He stood over her while she wrote a note to William, explaining her sudden disappearance. Miranda would understand when she heard the news. And Vangelis . . . well, it didn't really matter, did it, whether Vangelis understood or not?

As the taxi taking Anna and Justin to the airport passed the dig, Anna kept her head down in the car. She didn't want any of them to see her. Writing the letter to William had been hard enough. Saying goodbye in person would be impossible.

Six hours after making the decision to quit Crete and return to England with Justin, Anna was boarding a flight home. While they waited in the departure lounge, Justin slipped off to buy Anna a gift. It was a tiny replica of an ancient Minoan vase. Anna unwrapped it and smiled in thanks, though inside, the gift hit her heart like a dagger. Just one more week and they would definitely have found something like this perfect little pot.

'Bet you'll be glad to get back to civilisation,' said Justin as the plane climbed to twenty thousand feet. 'I mean, Crete is a beautiful island and all that, but what can you do with yourself there once you've looked at the view? Heraklion is a dump. There are no decent restaurants and no clubs. Still, I suppose I should be grateful that you didn't get to spend your nights trying to pull the locals.'

Anna smiled distantly and looked out of her window at the coastline of the island gradually disappearing into the horizon.

'It was all right,' she told him. 'We found plenty to do.'

'Well, there'll be plenty to do when we get back to London. I've arranged for us to go to dinner with Andy and Carina on Friday. Andy's just got a fantastic job with Wellard Brooker. Thinks he might be able to point them in my direction if they need another man. Seventy-five thousand a year basic,' he said, like an excited little boy. 'And bonuses twice a year. Andy told me that last year, one of their guys made three hundred and fifty K in bonuses alone.'

But Anna was only half listening. The figures Justin spoke of were unreal, dizzying.

'You'll be back to work tomorrow?' she asked, when he finally drew breath.

'Of course. Listen, thanks for not being difficult today, darling. It will make things so much easier for me if I don't have to take another day off.'

Then the NO SMOKING sign pinged off again and the stewards and stewardesses began to glide down the aisles with their trolleys. Anna thought she recognised the steward serving her and Justin. He was the one that Miranda had flirted with all those weeks ago.

'So, tell me about the other people on the dig,' Justin began, with a mouthful of airline chicken.

Anna opened her mouth to tell him, but before she could get much further than their names, the film started and Justin patted her on the arm and said, 'Tell me later on.'

Chapter Twenty-Two

Anna's flat hadn't changed at all. When she opened the door, the still air inside billowed out and enveloped her like the arms of a ghost. Junk mail was piled high on the doormat. Her plants, which Justin had promised to keep fed and watered while she was away, had long since died and shrivelled into little brown twigs.

Anna picked up the post and tossed most of it straight into the dustbin. Then she walked to her answer-machine. No light. No messages. She put the kettle on to make a cup of tea, realised that she had no milk, then turned the kettle off again.

She finally came to rest on the window sill, looking down on the dustbins belonging to the flat below. The lid had come off one of them and an alley cat, or maybe even an urban fox, had scattered chicken bones and fast-food cartons halfway up the street.

Yep, nothing much had changed in London. The same grey weather, casting a grey light over its grey buildings and grey people. Even the cat that meowed plaintively outside her neighbours' door was grey and unfriendly. Unlike the pretty little kittens in Crete.

Leaning against the window-frame, with her forehead pressed against the cold glass, Anna wondered what reaction there had been to her letter. She had expected to find some kind of acknowledgement of its receipt when she got back. An email or text at least. Perhaps they were glad to see the back of her. Anna sniffed hard as a tear breached her lashes and began to roll down her cheeks.

I would have had to come home in a week anyway, she told herself. And I wanted to be with Justin. I know I did. I hardly stopped thinking about him while I was out there. So why do I feel so bad now?

She picked up the phone to call him. What she was experiencing was just a dose of the post-holiday blues. A natural reaction to being plunged into the grey grimness of an English summer after all those weeks in the sun. Hearing Justin's voice would cheer her up again. Remind her of what she had in London that she could never have over there in Crete.

'Justin Leonard's office,' said his prompt, efficient secretary. Anna had never actually met the girl, but the clipped sound of her voice always made Anna feel as though she was just ringing up to waste Justin's time.

'Is Justin there?' she squeaked.

'Can I ask who's calling please?'

'It's Anna. It's his girlfriend.'

'One moment.' The secretary didn't put her on

hold, but merely held her hand across the mouth-piece as she enquired after Justin's availability.

'Tell her I'll call her later,' she heard him say in an ineffective whisper. 'I'm busy right now.' Then the tinkling of laughter. Whatever he was busy with, it sounded like fun.

'He's busy,' said the secretary. Anna hung up without saying goodbye. Outside, the first spots of a summer rainstorm hit the window. It seemed so hugely symbolic of the way Anna was feeling right then that she could no longer hold her tears inside.

All her hopes, all the optimism she had tenta-tively carried with her when she travelled out to Crete had been misplaced. Her adventure hadn't changed anything. Justin hadn't changed at all. It was still work first and her firmly in second place, even now that she had probably ballsed up her own career for good to be by his side. Slowly it dawned on her that it was more than her career she had given up.

Just then, her mobile rang. Anna picked it up eagerly, expecting to hear Justin's voice. If he said he would take her out to dinner, she told herself, she would forgive him for not putting her first that morning. But it wasn't Justin.

'Damn bloody nuisance, running off like that.' It was Dr Sillery. 'Typical of you to lose faith in us on the day that everything sorted itself out. Saw you driving off in that bloody taxi while I was coming back to the villa to tell you the good news.'

'What's that?' Anna shouted into the phone. The line from Crete was terrible.

'The news that we've found what we were looking for at last. We've struck gold, my dear. Miranda and I found a vase almost identical to the fake one. For real this time. I had it checked out in Athens. And the hotel authorities have agreed to give us another three months to finish the dig. Seems like I was right all along. It's going to be bigger than Knossos. And you could have been in on it all, you fool. Still can be in on it if you like.'

'What?'

'I'm asking you if you want to come back out and join us, you idiot. It's not often I go grovelling to people who write such badly punctuated letters of resignation, but the fact is, I don't trust anyone else. And everybody misses you,' he added.

'What? Everybody?'

'Well, maybe I don't miss you quite as much as everyone else.' It wasn't quite the right answer, but Anna knew that she wouldn't get from William the kind of emotional flannel she needed right then.

'So are you coming back?' he asked once more.

Anna looked out of the window at the driving rain and told him yes with no hesitation at all.

Leaving Justin a letter that would explain all and free him to do as much overtime as he wanted to, for ever, Anna caught a taxi back to the airport. She didn't much care this time that she would be flying out to Crete on a charter flight full of noisy holiday-makers. Instead, she was buoyed up by their excitement. She, too, was looking forward to touching down in the sun.

*   *   *

'Great place for a holiday,' said the woman who was sitting next to her.

'Yes.' Anna nodded. 'Though I'm going out there to work.'

'Work? Lucky you. Beats working in some office, I bet.'

'Yes,' said Anna. It did beat working in some office. In fact, it beat working in England, full stop.

'You got a boyfriend out there?' the woman asked.

'No. Though I have got my eye on someone special.'

'Greek god?' asked the woman.

'You can say that again.'

But as the plane began to circle Heraklion airport, waiting for a moment to land, Anna found herself growing nervous. What if she was setting herself up for more heartache? William had said that everyone was missing her, but surely that was just a figure of speech . . .

Anna started to shake with nerves as she followed the snaking line of passengers to the baggage hall and picked up her hurriedly repacked bag. In the arrivals lounge, new arrivals swarmed around the hassled young tour reps. Anna looked out for the driver to take her back to the villa but could see no one with a card bearing her name.

Chapter Twenty-Three

Soon the airport arrivals hall had emptied. There was no one left in the vast cold room but Anna and a cleaner, who swept away the rubbish with acute boredom on his face. Anna was about to ask him where she could catch a taxi when the automatic doors to the car park slid open behind her.

Anna turned slowly, like a movie heroine about to experience a great dramatic moment. Even as she turned, she began to get a sense of who she would find behind her. The smell of his familiar cologne wafted towards her on the warm night air. Vangelis had come for her. Now he stood in the doorway, like a mirage. Anna picked up her bag and started to walk towards him.

It was a walk that seemed to take for ever. With every step, Anna expected him to disappear into mid-air and leave her walking towards nothing but the night. But Vangelis didn't disappear, and as she neared him, he opened his arms in welcome. Anna dropped her bag then, and ran the last few feet to leap into his embrace.

'I thought I had lost you for ever,' she said.

Vangelis said nothing, but began to kiss her. Warm, passionate kisses that pushed away the last grey memories of life in London. They might have stayed there for ever, kissing like that, but soon another plane landed and another crowd of tourists came pushing through the barrier. Vangelis retrieved Anna's bag and led her quickly to the car.

He drove as though the devil were on his tail to get Anna back to the villa. As they turned into the familiar driveway, Anna felt herself flooded with warmth. A candle lamp was burning in the porch to light her way back. Anna skipped her way up the pathway, stopping only to smell the pretty pink flowers which had charmed her so much on her first morning.

'Miranda! William!' she called as Vangelis unlocked the door and let her inside.

'They are not here,' he told her. 'They thought that we might like to be alone for a while.'

Anna smiled and couldn't stop herself from blushing. Miranda and William knew. Everyone had known how Anna felt about Vangelis except Anna herself. She felt a little stupid that it had taken a flight back to London and the prospect of never seeing him again to convince her of the fact.

Vangelis shrugged. 'You do want to be alone with me, don't you?'

Anna laughed. 'Of course I do.'

Soon they were back in her bedroom and standing at the foot of her cool, wide bed. The lipstick she had so carefully applied during landing in the hope of seeing him at the airport was quickly kissed away. Then he moved on to her neck. Her biscuit-brown shoulders. To the beautiful hollow where her neck slid smoothly into her collarbone. Anna, meanwhile, ran her hands all over Vangelis's heavenly body. She trailed her fingers feverishly through his thick curly hair, grazed her fingertips gently over the stubble on his cheeks, and felt the hard outline of his muscles beneath the crisp cotton of his shirt.

The warm scent of his nut-brown skin filled her nostrils and her lungs. And soon she could smell her own perfume billowing up from her body as her flesh grew warmer with excitement. Then suddenly – inexplicably – Anna felt her eyes begin to prickle with the first warning of impending tears.

She tried to choke them back, fumbling with the buttons of Vangelis's loose white cotton shirt, but having no luck with her eyes so full of tears, gave up and instead helped him pull the shirt off over his head still buttoned up. His hands slid up her leg beneath her flimsy skirt until he found the edge of her knickers and pushed them out of the way.

Anna clutched at his shoulders as Vangelis leaned his full weight on her to make her lie down on the bed. She sighed again as she felt his fingers make contact with her bare flesh. He found the right place instantly and started to massage, bringing his hand away once to lick his fingers so that the friction would tease but not burn.

Still the tears coursed down Anna's face. Vangelis could taste them salty on her lips when he kissed her.

'Are you sad?' he murmured.

She shook her head firmly. She wasn't sad at all.

Vangelis's fingers twisted in hers, holding her hands above her head as they moved together towards the climax. And what a powerful climax it would be. Anna could feel it gathering inside her, like a wave waiting to burst through a flood barrier. Her whole body shivered with anticipation, clothed in an aura of electricity waiting to gather itself into a ball of rapturous lightning at her hub.

'I love you,' he murmured, and it finally pushed her over the edge. Tears and orgasm, all coming at once. Anna was racked by her desire, and love, and relief. As Vangelis came inside her, she called out his name, and knew that she no longer had to feel guilty.

Lying silently on the bed in the early hours of the next morning, Anna listened to the sound of the sea caressing the shore. In the bed beside her, Vangelis was still sleeping, the soft sound of his breathing echoing the whisper of the sea. The light of the moon filtering in through the thin white curtains was just enough to see him by. His gentle face, his curly black hair spread out across the pillow like the mane of a horse in the wind.

How had she failed to noticed that he was beautiful before? she asked herself. She knew he was handsome, sure. But now she knew she had seen him as he really was, all guards dropped, naked and vulnerable in the bed beside her.

He had given her everything. There would be no games with him as there had been with Justin. No pretending to feel less for each other than they actually did in a misguided attempt at self-protection.

Suddenly, Anna knew that she was where she was supposed to be. Here was someone who loved and wanted everything about her. Here was someone who would never be disgruntled when she had dirt beneath her nails from digging . . .

Suddenly, Anna laughed. The relief exploded from her with as much delicious power as any orgasm.

Vangelis stirred, sat upright, surprised.

'What? What?' he asked. 'What is the matter?'

'Nothing,' said Anna soothingly. 'Nothing at all. I was just thinking that since I'm sticking around I ought to learn the Greek for "I love you".'

Want more from Stephanie Ash . . . ?

The First Kiss

Stephanie Ash

He tangled loving fingers in her beautiful hair and fixed her eyes with his most penetrating gaze . . .

Amelia Ashton is a woman with ambition. A singer-songwriter determined to make it to the top of the music business, she finds her plans going awry as one record producer after another falls for her long red hair rather than her sweet music.

When an invitation to her American mother's fifth wedding in Las Vegas arrives, Amelia decides to take a break from them all while she does her daughterly duty, but a chance meeting with an old friend makes for a surprisingly interesting trip. And when Amelia returns to London she is more than ready to sort out her affairs, both musical and otherwise . . .

Out from Sphere in February 2013.

One More Kiss

Stephanie Ash

His hands weren't quite so gentle now . . .

Amelia Ashton has made it. The singer-songwriter
is one of the biggest recording stars of her time –
but the success she has longed for has taken its toll
and her life is no longer her own.

When she goes AWOL from her sell-out tour of
the US, Amelia heads back to London in search
of some quality time. Meeting up with Karis,
her former girlfriend-in-crime, Amelia is soon in
the midst of some sensual adventures, such as
consummating a childhood crush at her friend's
wedding. And furthering her career in a most
unexpected way . . .

Out from Sphere in February 2013.